He sighed.

'I *am* attending
I am not a rela
you were as I
Barleyfields in my absence, or should I say attempting to.'

Leah stared at him in horror. It was the absent perfectionist. Nathan Bonner had returned to Barleyfields within minutes of her taking over.

Dear Reader

Autumn books to warm the heart! Gideon really believes he has NOTHING LEFT TO GIVE until Beth proves him wrong, in Caroline Anderson's latest story. Their past relationship makes Alison and Grant decide to be STRICTLY PROFESSIONAL in work, according to Laura MacDonald. Abigail Gordon's CALMER WATERS and Judith Ansell's HIS SHELTERING ARMS are equally touching. We think you'll love these stories.

The Editor

!!!STOP PRESS!!! If you enjoy reading these medical books, have you ever thought of writing one? We are always looking for new writers for LOVE ON CALL, and want to hear from you. Send for the guidelines, with SAE, and start writing!

Abigail Gordon began writing some years ago at the suggestion of her sister, who is herself an established writer. She has found it an absorbing and fulfilling way of expressing herself, and feels that in the medical romance there is an opportunity to present realistically strong dramatic situations with which readers can identify. Abigail lives in a Cheshire village near Stockport, and is widowed with three grown-up sons, and several grandchildren.

Recent titles by the same author:

NO SHADOW OF DOUBT
JOEL'S WAY

CALMER WATERS

BY
ABIGAIL GORDON

MILLS & BOON

MILLS & BOON LIMITED
ETON HOUSE, 18-24 PARADISE ROAD
RICHMOND, SURREY TW9 1SR

*All the characters in this book have no existence outside the imagina-
tion of the Author, and have no relation whatsoever to anyone bearing
the same name or names. They are not even distantly inspired by any
individual known or unknown to the Author, and all the incidents
are pure invention.*

*MILLS & BOON, the Rose Device and LOVE ON CALL
are trademarks of the publisher.*

*First published in Great Britain 1994
by Mills & Boon Limited*

© Abigail Gordon 1994

*Australian copyright 1994   Philippine copyright 1994
This edition 1994*

ISBN 0 263 78829 6

Set in Times 10 on 11 pt.

03-9410-51784

Made and printed in Great Britain

CHAPTER ONE

'YES, I think you will suit us very nicely, my dear,' the woman behind the desk said. 'My son is the actual owner of Barleyfields,' she told the erect young figure sitting opposite, 'but at the moment he's on a lecture tour of the Netherlands and I don't want to concern him with problems at this end. I've taken it upon myself to employ someone in Denise's place, and as you come highly recommended from St Bridget's, have had experience in geriatric nursing, and I like the look of you, I'm prepared to offer you the position. It hasn't been advertised as yet, and I feel if I can make the appointment without all that preamble it will serve the best purpose all round.'

Leah's heart lifted. To be employed as sister-in-charge of Barleyfields Nursing Home for the Elderly, with an attractive apartment on the premises, would be the answer to all her problems.

Celia Bonner's smile was rueful. 'I've lived in Spain for many years,' she explained, 'and I'm finding the English spring a little too chilly for my liking. I will be glad to get back.'

She was small, still faintly tanned from the Spanish winter, and very smart, and Leah couldn't help but admire the way this elderly woman had flown in with all speed to deal with the predicament at Barleyfields.

Denise Myers had held the position previously, but at the present time she was a patient in Women's Surgical at St Bridget's Hospital nearby where Leah was ward sister.

She had been involved in a motor accident two weeks before and had received multiple fractures, and when

5

Leah had been chatting to her the previous day, the injured woman had said wanly, 'One thing is for sure: I won't be going back to Barleyfields. It will be months before I'm mobile again, and even then the work will be too hard after all this, and on top of that my Bill wouldn't let me. I've just had a visit from Mrs Bonner, the lady who's running things at present, and I've told her she'll have to replace me.'

Leah had noticed that the woman who had just left had seemed serious and preoccupied, and now Denise had come up with a reason.

'Did you live in?' she asked, only mildly curious.

'No. I have my own house near the home, but I could have done if I'd wanted. There's a lovely flat on the top floor.'

'Really?' Leah's interest was expanding. 'That's interesting. I'm looking for a position with living accommodation. I'm in the nurses' residences at the moment, but someone is coming to live with me in the near future, and hospital hours and a bedsit in the nurses' home aren't going to be the right sort of set-up.'

'The hours wouldn't be any shorter at Barleyfields,' Denise had cautioned, 'and living on the premises can make one just that bit too available.'

'Yes, I know that,' Leah had agreed, 'but I'd be willing to put up with that for the sake of somewhere decent to live.'

The plump forty-year-old in the bed had eyed the slender figure of the ward sister.

'Have you done any geriatric nursing?'

Leah had shaken her head with its dark gloss of unruly waves in mock anguish. 'Indeed I have, and I've got the temperamental back that goes with it.'

'Haven't we all?' the other woman said with a wry smile.

*　　*　　*

As a result of that conversation with Denise she had rung Barleyfields, and after a moment's surprised silence Mrs Bonner had suggested that she go round there at the end of her shift at St Bridget's.

It was a clear, cold afternoon. A mischievous breeze teased the branches of the trees and bullied the daffodils into a reluctant quivering dance. Small clouds scudded across a pale sky, and as the big stone house came into view at the end of a winding drive, Leah felt the excitement that comes with a new venture.

She stopped her small car and looked around her. When she had been small, the mill manager had lived there, and after him other well-to-do folks, but now an enterprising family had turned Barleyfields into a nursing home for the elderly and she was interested to see inside.

'You'll observe that we're not a very big concern,' Celia Bonner said as she took Leah on a tour of inspection before interviewing her. 'Forty patients at the most. There are much larger homes in the area, but Barleyfields has a reputation second to none. My son insists on high standards of care, and is very particular when choosing staff.'

'I see,' Leah said slowly, blue eyes grave. Would he approve of her, she wondered, if his mother should offer her the job?

The rooms were bright and airy, the furnishings solid but tasteful, and there was an abundance of sanitary arrangements, plus a large kitchen and even bigger laundry.

Old eyes followed them round, some bright with curiosity, others blank, and some not even seeing them, so engrossed were they in their own thoughts.

There was nothing depressing about Barleyfields. It was a tranquil sort of place, and as she observed the house and its residents Leah felt that, just as in caring for the sick on a surgical ward, there was equal job

satisfaction to be found from making the last years of
the elderly as happy as possible.

And now they were in the small office situated off the
main hallway, and after having asked for details of
Leah's career to date in health care, Celia Bonner
offered her the position of sister-in-charge at
Barleyfields.

'So what do you say, Miss Morgan?' she asked. 'You
tell me that you're single, which is always an advantage
in this sort of situation. It's clear that you like the flat
and its furnishings, and you say that you were brought
up in this area so you're familiar with the surroundings,
so. . .?'

Leah knew she did not have to think about her
answer, but there was one thing she had to clarify first.

'Would your son have any objection to someone
sharing the flat with me?' she asked, not wanting to
get off on the wrong foot with the absent perfectionist.

'In what capacity?' the other woman asked. 'Lover?
Friend? Relative?'

Leah's face twisted. Lover? Never that! Not now.

'It's a relative,' she explained. 'I'm shortly going to
be responsible for my young sister.'

'I don't see that being a problem as long as the child
is kept under control,' Celia Bonner said, and as Leah's
steady blue gaze met hers, she thought that the girl
was quite beautiful in a subdued sort of way, and then
she smiled, a bright beam of pleasure, and there wasn't
the least doubt about it. . . Leah Morgan *was*
beautiful.

'Then in that case I'd like to accept your offer,'
she said. 'I'm anxious to get away from hospital
life because of the situation with my sister, but didn't
want to hand in my notice until I'd found another
position.'

Mrs Bonner smiled her approval of Leah's acceptance, but there was curiosity in her eyes.

'Good,' she said briskly. 'I'm pleased that you're coming to join us. How soon can you start? I appreciate that you'll have to work your notice at St Bridget's. As you say, it would have been imprudent to jettison one position without having another to replace it, unless, of course, you have private means.'

Leah's smile disappeared. Her face was bleak. It *would* have been risky. . .too risky, as for one thing she *didn't* have private means. The days were gone when she was prepared to take chances. She had lived with the master when it came to doing that, and seen where it had got him. . .and her.

'The nursing manager at St Bridget's knows my circumstances,' she said quietly, 'and as I still have three weeks' holiday entitlement owing to me, and I will be moving into another part of health care where the need is quite acute, I'm pretty sure that she will let me finish at the end of the week instead of working the usual month's notice.'

Celia Bonner clapped her hands.

'Marvellous! I could show you the ropes on Monday morning and book a lunchtime flight back to Spain. Shall I have a word with your nursing manager to explain the position here?'

'Yes, if you would,' Leah agreed, 'although she has promised that there would be no delay if I found a suitable position. Luckily she has a member of staff due back any time from maternity leave.' Her smile flashed out again. 'I consider myself very fortunate to have found something so suitable so soon.'

'I think that it will be fortunate for Barleyfields, too,' the older woman said, and Leah's heart lifted again. The way ahead was clearer now, and apart from Katie it was a road she was going to travel alone. No tempting diversions, no seeing rainbows when storm clouds were gathering, or taking glib promises to be signposts to happiness; just a long straight slog until she'd found her self-respect again.

'I've got the job at Barleyfields,' Leah told Denise next morning when she arrived on the ward after a meeting with the nursing manager. 'St Bridget's are letting me finish at the end of the week.'

'Great,' she murmured drowsily, having been sedated after a painful and restless night.

'The man who owns the place. . . Mrs Bonner's son. . .sounds rather intimidating. What's he like?' Leah asked.

Denise's eyes were closing, but she managed a sleepy chuckle.

'A force to be reckoned with. We call him the Great Nate. He'll expect nothing less than a curtsy from you when you're presented to him, so be prepared, but that shouldn't be for a while; he's abroad at the moment.'

Leah laughed.

'Oh, yes? And touch my forelock, too?'

'Yes, that too,' Denise murmured before slipping into sleep, and with those few words Leah had to be content, for later in the day the injured woman was transferred to the special fractures unit at St Bernadette's, the sister hospital to St Bridget's.

Leah had laughed at the description of her future employer, but there was unease inside her. Did she want to be under the heel of a tyrant? Better that than to be enmeshed in the machinations of a plausible thief, she decided bitterly, and as the never-ending demands of Women's Surgical took over she had no further time to worry about the absent lecturer. She would do the job at Barleyfields efficiently and without fuss, just as she did at St Bridget's, and, that being so, should have little need for contact with the Bonner man.

*   *   *

That night Leah rang Toronto and when her father's breezy voice came over the line she gave a wry smile. She loved him dearly, but there were times when she wished that Jack Morgan would think a bit more before he acted.

A jovial fair-haired widower in his late forties, he had suddenly presented his two daughters with a new stepmother, along with the news that his firm were transferring him to their Canadian plant for a twelve-month period.

Their mother, Diana, had died during a kidney operation only a short time previously, and although Leah had expected that her father would not be long without a woman in his life, she had been taken aback by the speed with which he'd filled the empty space.

It had been easier to accept once she had met Elise, who was to be their new stepmother, for she was a pleasant, attractive woman whose feet were firmly on the ground, and obviously devoted to their charming father. What was more, she had been at great pains to make it clear that she had no wish to supplant the memory of their much loved mother.

The estimable Elise had also been prepared to start her married life in a strange country with her new husband, and was willing to take Katie, his youngest daughter, with them.

Leah had not been very happy about the arrangement. She and Katie were very close, especially since losing their mother, and she had remonstrated with her father that such a move could prove traumatic for her younger sister, and for Elise, who had never had children of her own.

But Jack had just laughed, and assured her, 'It'll be all right, Leah, you'll see. Why don't you come with us and then I'll have all my womenfolk under one roof?'

She had glared at him.

'Really, Dad! Elise hasn't been married before!

Give her a chance. I certainly don't want to play gooseberry.'

'What you're really saying is that you don't want to leave Terry,' he had teased. 'That's more like the truth.'

'Maybe,' she had parried back, 'but that doesn't mean that I won't have Katie with me at the cottage instead of her being uprooted.'

'Stop fussing, Leah,' he had told her. 'She'll love it over there. What could be more exciting for a youngster than going to live in a new country?'

'She's the wrong age, Dad,' she had argued. 'Katie will be leaving all her friends behind, and at thirteen they're the most important people in a kid's life, and added to that, although Elise is lovely, Katie hardly knows her.'

The set, mulish look that he always adopted when he was not getting his own way had settled on her father's face and he had growled, 'She's going, and that's it, Leah. Katie's dead set on it, and we're not changing our plans at this late stage.'

That had been eight months ago, and it was only recently that Leah had discovered how right she had been. A tearful phone call from Katie begging to come back because she was homesick and hated the kids at her new school was followed by a sheepish confirmation of the situation by her father. It had resulted in Leah's having to rearrange her life for a second time in just a few months.

By that time her cottage had been sold so that Terry could repay the money he had embezzled from his employers to stay out of prison. Her affection for him had turned to loathing, and yet she had not been able to stand by and see him gaoled as he surely would have been, it not being his first offence. And with him long gone she had moved into hospital accommodation as she could not afford anything else.

With the man she had thought she loved gone from her life, and her family in Toronto, Leah had felt ashamed and lonely. The shame was for her gullibility in letting a handsome face and impeccable manners blind her to Terry's unscrupulousness. The news that Katie wanted to come home had been the first ray of light in her misery, and she had promised the weepy young girl that the moment she found suitable accommodation they would be together.

A chance remark from a patient in her care had helped her to do just that, and as her father listened to her news and agreed to book a flight for Katie to come home the moment she gave the word, Leah began to feel that order was coming back to her life.

As she undressed beside her narrow bed later that night she caught sight of herself in the mirror, and for some reason Denise's warning came into her mind. She formed her features into an expression of extreme deference, and then in her pearly nakedness curtsied deeply, holding herself in the position until she toppled over into a laughing heap.

'I'm getting my act together, Mr Bonner, sir,' she giggled, and then, on a more serious note, 'Barleyfields, here I come!'

Celia Bonner showed Leah the various functions of the small office off the main hall that would be hers: the drugs cupboard; patients' records; staff rotas; the procedure for accepting, prior to banking, the fees from those residents who were not funded by Social Services; details of the various GPs available if required; and a myriad other small functions that went towards the smooth running of Barleyfields.

Leah was then introduced to the staff on duty, which consisted of two RGNs, three care assistants, a rather supercilious-looking young man who turned out to be the cook, and two middle-aged women cleaners, and been received with varying degrees of enthusiasm.

After that she met the patients, greeted initially with an abrupt, 'And who might you be, then?' from a fierce-looking old lady in a tweed skirt and lambswool jumper.

And on her heels a small gnome-like man leaning heavily on a stick had surveyed her with twinkling eyes and said, 'Pleased to meet you, my dear. What's for lunch?'

So it had gone on until they arrived back in the office, where Celia Bonner had announced, 'Obviously my son is in charge of Barleyfields, and once he gets back you'll be able to consult him on all matters that concern you, Leah. In the meantime, it will be up to you. You'll find that most of the staff are excellent and they'll help you out if you get stuck.'

She glanced at the expensive watch on her thin wrist. 'And now I must fly. . .literally. I'm on a four o'clock flight. It will be marvellous to get back to my own home. I've been staying in Nathan's house while I've been here, which is fine, but I'm afraid that at my age one becomes very much a creature of habit.'

When she had gone, Leah looked around her. She was feeling happier than she had been in months. Taking charge of Barleyfields was a challenge and she was determined to meet it with all the skill and determination she possessed. Once Katie arrived, it would be just the two of them and the job. That would be all she needed. No distractions from the opposite sex. She had had her fill of them.

At that moment, three things happened simultaneously. An old man bent against the chill wind went past the office window, dressed in just a cardigan and baggy cord trousers.

Giles, the cook, appeared in the doorway and

announced laconically, 'Mary's flooded the bathroom at the end of the passage again.'

And a taxi came slowly up the drive.

Leah swung round to face him.

'Where are the rest of the staff?' she asked quickly.

'On lunch, or seeing to the folks upstairs,' he said with the same lack of urgency.

'Right,' she said crisply. 'You go and fetch the man who's just going down the drive, and I'll deal with the bathroom.'

'Not an escapee!' he exclaimed in mock horror, but Leah was not listening.

She ran down the passage towards where water was pouring over the side of the bath like a miniature Niagara, watched with a childlike sort of fascination by the offending Mary.

As she flung herself towards the taps, Leah did not see the soap on the tiles, and as she stepped on it, her feet shot from under her and she landed in a heap on the wet floor. She groaned. The water was seeping through her crisp blue uniform, and she had scraped her elbow on the side of the bath. The fall had knocked the wind out of her, and she lay there for a moment gathering her wits, quite unaware that she was being observed by a pair of amazed brown eyes. In the panic of the moment, she had not heard the door slam or heavy footsteps hurrying along the hallway to investigate the commotion.

When a man's deep voice asked testily, 'What is going on here, Nurse?' Leah sat up and began to struggle to her feet with as much dignity as she could muster. His arm came out to assist her, but she shrugged it off, angry with herself for being caught in such an undignified position by a visitor. He turned off the taps, stepping precariously through the water in a pair of expensive-looking leather brogues, and there was nothing left for her to do but clean up and let him make his way to whoever it was he had come to visit.

Leah managed to drag up a smile.

'It was just a hiccup. All part of a day's work. Who have you come to see?'

The man smiled back, and she thought that he had a strong mouth with a full lower lip above a firm chin. His hair was thick dark russet and needed cutting, as it lay heavy on his brow and above his ears. He made no attempt to answer the question. He had one of his own.

'Where's Denise?' The curtness of his tone belied the smile.

'In hospital,' she informed him with equal brevity.

'So who's in charge?'

'I am.'

'And who are you?'

'Leah Morgan, and I really must ask you to go about your business while I clean up here, as I'm anxious to change into a clean uniform.'

He sighed.

'I *am* attending to my business, Leah Morgan. I am not a relative of a patient. I asked who you were as I need to know who is running Barleyfields in my absence, or should I say, attempting to.'

Leah stared at him in horror. It was the absent perfectionist. Nathan Bonner had returned to Barleyfields within minutes of her taking over.

'You're Nathan Bonner,' she said weakly.

'Yes, I am. I've just flown in from Holland, and I'm more than ready for a bath and a shave, but it looks as if my requirements will have to be put on hold until I've sorted this. . .'

Leah looked round frantically for something to wipe up the floor and he broke off what he was saying to growl irritably, 'Leave that. The cleaners will see to it.'

'They've gone,' she told him.

'All right, but there's one of those Vax things some-where in the place. One of the others can do it; I'd like a word with you in the office.'

Leah's inside clenched. She was going to get the sack before she had even started. And what about Katie?

There was worse to come. He was leading the way into the office when the front door was flung open and Giles appeared holding the elderly absconder firmly by the arm. When the young cook saw Nathan Bonner he looked surprised and then he grinned. 'Hi, Mr Bonner. So you're back?'

'Yes, and not before time, it would appear. Where have you been?'

'Old Charlie here was doing his daily escape routine,' he explained, and as Leah and Nathan Bonner eyed him in dismay, Giles said, 'There's no cause for alarm. He never goes farther than the farm at the top of the road. Used to be a farmer himself. They let him help with the milking.'

Before Leah could voice her thoughts, the man at her side was saying them for her.

'There'll be cause for alarm if he gets pneumonia from going out not properly protected against the cold, and even more so if he should get knocked down or lost!' He turned to Leah and she felt herself cringing against the anger in the tawny eyes. 'It just won't do, Sister,' and, giving the unabashed Giles a brief nod, he propelled her into the office.

Leah braced herself. She was not going to go down without a fight. Nathan Bonner was going to have to be told that none of this was her fault, that she had been thrown in at the deep end, and given the chance would show him that she was capable, efficient, and. . .

'Stay there!' he commanded, and strode off into the kitchen, leaving her to wonder if he'd gone to see if there was anything else he could find fault with before he dressed her down.

He was back within seconds carrying a bowl of warm water, lint, and antiseptic ointment, and as she stared at him in surprise he said, 'You've hurt your arm. Let me see.'

She held it out reluctantly, thinking that this encounter was going from bad to worse. He was bathing her wounds before sending her packing. His touch was gentle and impersonal, and when he'd finished, he said briskly, 'You're lucky. It's just a bad graze, no bones broken. If there had been I'd have had to take you to St Bernadette's to patch you up.'

Brilliant blue eyes widened.

'Why? What are you?'

It was his turn to stare.

'A doctor, of course. Orthopaedic surgeon, to be exact.'

Her jaw dropped. His mother had said he was on a lecture tour, and for some reason she'd guessed him to be an academic or industrialist type of person, certainly not in health care like herself.

'And now that we've cleared the air as to my status in life, I think we might discuss yours here at Barleyfields,' he said, seating himself behind the desk that she'd been told was hers. 'Who gave you the position here?'

'Your mother.'

He raised bushy bronze eyebrows, one slightly higher than the other.

'My mother! She actually managed to tear herself away from her Spanish villa?'

'Yes,' she said quietly. 'Denise was badly injured in a car accident and your mother came over to keep an eye on things, and to find a replacement as Denise won't be coming back. She told me that you were away, and she didn't want to bother you with problems at this end. When I came for an interview she offered me the position. She only flew back to Spain this afternoon.'

'So I've missed her,' he said regretfully.

'Yes, I'm afraid so.'

The inquisition wasn't over

'And what were you doing before you came here?'

'I was sister on Women's Surgical at St Bridget's. Denise was one of my patients, and that's how I heard about the vacancy here.'

The tawny eyes were giving nothing away.

'I see,' he said thoughtfully. 'And how long have you been here?'

This was her moment and she wasn't going to blow it.

'I started this morning. Your mother left me in charge just ten minutes before you arrived.'

If she'd expected apologies or commiserations about the disastrous start to her employment at Barleyfields, Leah was to be disappointed. After one second of startled amazement he got to his feet and said blandly, 'You're learning fast, then. In just a short space of time, you've discovered we have a wanderer and a water fetishist. . .and a travel-stained orthopaedic surgeon.' And on that note he departed, leaving her to gather her wits.

CHAPTER TWO

'THAT was bad luck, Sister, Nathan Bonner arriving back from Holland just as you'd taken over,' one of the young auxiliary nurses said, when Leah ventured forth from the office. 'I've got rid of most of the water, but it's quite damp everywhere.'

She was a tall, slim girl with long fair hair in a ponytail and an open, friendly face, and Leah took an instant liking to her.

'Yes, well, that particular bathroom will have to be a no-go area until it dries out I'm afraid, and Mary supervised whenever she has to use any of the other bathrooms,' Leah said quietly, 'and you must excuse me, but I've been introduced to so many people I can't just recall your name.'

'It's Suzanne, but everybody calls me Suzie,' she said with a smile.

Leah smiled back.

'Suzie it is, then. I won't forget again, and now I think I'd better start earning my keep, but first of all, as I'm rather damp myself, I need to go and change,' she said with a rueful glance at her saturated hemline.

'Fancy the boss finding you swimming around in the sluice,' a voice said from behind, with a hard little laugh, and Leah turned to find the younger of the two RGNs behind her.

'Sister wasn't in the sluice,' Suzie protested. 'It was in the bathroom.'

'Wherever it was, I'll bet he took a dim view of it,' the other woman countered.

Leah could recognise antagonism when she saw it.

'And you are?' she asked evenly.

'Annette Pryce. I work regular days, and I've been more or less running the place since Denise had her accident.'

'And so why didn't you apply for the position?' Leah asked in the same even tone.

'Because Nathan insists it should be a sister-in-charge.'

'And that's exactly what I am, but it shouldn't stop us from being friends, Annette. I'd be grateful to hear anything you can tell me about the running of Barleyfields,' she said tactfully.

Her antagonist was a striking redhead, small, slim, with calculating green eyes, and as the woman eyed her consideringly, Leah knew that unless she could win her round, Annette Pryce was going to be a thorn in her side.

It appeared there was to be a truce of sorts.

'Yes, all right,' she agreed grudgingly. 'Anything you want to know, just ask,' and she strode off down the hallway.

'Annette doesn't like anyone else to get a look in with Mr Bonner,' Suzie said. 'She's been itching for him to get back.'

Leah eyed her in surprise.

'He's not married, then?'

It was the young care assistant's turn to be surprised.

'No. Didn't you know?' She pointed to where a smart bungalow was just visible between the trees. 'He lives there on his own. He used to have the flat that you've got, but when he'd had the bungalow built he moved out.'

So the intimidating owner of Barleyfields was a bit of a loner, Leah thought, as she dashed upstairs to change. Her face tightened. That made two of them. Except for having Katie with her that was how she was going to be.

She hadn't noticed the bungalow in the grounds, and

it had been a shock to discover that he would be living
so near, but hopefully, apart from the occasional visit,
he would stay in his own house and be fully occupied
with the orthopaedic surgery that he was involved in,
while she was left to get on with the job she'd come
to do. If there was one thing she didn't want, it was
someone like Bonner looking over her shoulder all
the time.

Her cases were in the bedroom waiting to be
unpacked, and her spare uniforms were inside them,
so they were going to be somewhat creased. There was
no time to get out the iron. It was going to be a case
of changing from damp to crumpled.

When Leah came off duty at five o'clock, the soli-
tude of her new abode beckoned invitingly. It had been
a full day. She was now au fait with all the patients,
had noted their various medical requirements, and had
observed that there were two lounges at Barleyfields.
It appeared that those who were more agile physically
and mentally congregated in the one on the back that
overlooked green lawns and flowerbeds, while the less
alert patients gathered in the lounge on the front which
had a less inspiring view as it faced the drive and
visitors' car park.

The segregation seemed all wrong to her, and she
vowed that in the immediate future staff would be told
to mix the patients, so that those more feeble might
benefit from the stimulus of the fitter ones.

Giles, the laconic cook, had produced a well-
balanced evening meal for the residents that was
appetising and tastefully presented. It would be served
by the early evening staff who came in from five o'clock
until eight, when the night staff took over until eight
the following morning, and it had occurred to Leah
that Nathan Bonner had a formidable number of staff
on his payroll to provide the round-the-clock care that
was needed.

The flat was on the back of the house, and, when she let herself in, pale spring sunshine was filling the large lounge. She gazed around her with pleasure. So this was where her boss used to live. No wonder it was so attractively laid out. A small fitted kitchen led off the lounge, and at the other side of the entrance hall there was a large bedroom with twin beds, with a small, elegant bathroom en suite. The furnishings were expensive, the decor restful, and Leah thought she couldn't have chosen better herself.

She could see the roof of the Bonner man's bungalow down below, and she had to admit she was curious about the man with the nut-brown hair and the all-seeing eyes. Was he so difficult that no woman wanted him? she wondered. Hardly. Lots of women liked domineering men, and according to young Suzie Annette Pryce had the hots for him, and no doubt there were others. Or maybe he was choosy. Thought the woman for him had yet to be created.

Leah shrugged slim shoulders. She didn't really care one way or the other. Her affair with Terry Farnham had taken the edge off her appetite.

She had almost finished unpacking when there was a knock on the door. She'd told the evening staff to send for her if any emergencies arose, but hadn't expected it to be so soon. When she opened the door Nathan Bonner was standing firmly on the mat and as she eyed him apprehensively, he said crisply, 'I thought I'd better check to see if anyone had brought in some provisions for you.'

'Er—there are one or two odds and ends in the kitchen cupboard, and I've brought a loaf and a couple of tins of soup,' she said hurriedly as she let him in.

'Sounds rather frugal,' he commented, as he gazed around him.' My mother should have seen to it.'

Leah cleared her throat nervously.

'It's quite all right. I'm fine. When I finish work

tomorrow night I'll do a big shop. I know all the super-markets. I can manage for now. I've been unpacking, and as it's been quite a day I shall have an early night.'

'All right, if you say so,' he said abruptly, and then on a milder note, 'I used to live up here. Did you know?'

'Yes, someone did mention it. The furnishings are very attractive.'

'Hmm, you think so? I must admit that I rather went to town on it. I suppose it was because it was the first place I'd had to myself. Now I've got the bungalow, which is fine, but I'll always have a soft spot for this flat.'

While he'd been speaking Leah had been noting the features of him that she hadn't taken in at their disastrous encounter earlier in the day, and she had to admit that if she hadn't put herself on a strict diet of non-involvement she would be impressed with what she was seeing.

Nathan Bonner was of average height, average build, but it was clear that he was a far from average person. The strong mouth with its full lower lip, the tawny eyes and the thick brown crop flecked with copper would alone have lifted him from the ordinary, but added to that was the man's presence, the authority and confidence that emanated from him. She turned her head away. How was it Denise had described him? A force to be reckoned with? It would appear she'd been pretty accurate, and Leah hoped that she would be able to combat the force, as there was no way she wanted to join the ranks of the unemployed.

They had been observing each other. Nathan Bonner saw the slender curves of the newest member of his staff, the beautiful though melancholy face framed in the dark glossy hair. . .and the withdrawn expression as she turned away.

'What's the matter, Leah Morgan?' he asked with a tight smile. 'Am I making you nervous? I get the impression that you think I'm expecting you to bow the knee.'

The Leah of the pre-Terry era would have hooted with laughter at the suggestion that she might be nervous. She'd had pride and lots of confidence in all aspects of her life then, but now the only thing she was confident about was her job.

In recent months she'd experienced shame and poverty, and even though she hadn't been responsible for bringing it upon herself, it hadn't been any less painful. She'd been so proud of the cottage she'd bought in a small Cheshire village, and when she'd met Terry had generously let him share it with her. When he'd pleaded with her to sell it to keep him out of prison, it had been the worst moment of her life. She'd lost her trust and her home, and his degradation had washed off on to her.

'Well, are you?' Nathan Bonner repeated.

Leah had a sudden feeling that here was a man who liked straight talk. There was nothing forked about his tongue. He didn't beat about the bush and expected the same from others, and so she said, 'Yes, I am nervous. First of all, because I need to keep this job, and secondly, because Denise did warn me that you'd expect a display of subservience from me.'

She thought he might have laughed, or been annoyed, but instead he gave a disdainful snort and said drily, 'Did she, indeed? I don't recollect ever having asked my staff to humble themselves on my account. I'll have to have a word with that young woman. I'm told that she's been transferred to my fracture unit, and if she doesn't watch it she'll be getting a splint where she least expects it.'

He was smiling now, but she had a feeling that he wasn't too pleased, and on a quick change of subject she said, 'I don't suppose *your* cupboards had been stocked up either?'

He nodded ruefully.

'No, but that's what comes of arriving unannounced. As a matter of fact, I'm going down the road for a take-away, and then tomorrow, like yourself, I shall get organised. At this precise moment, jet-lag seems to be catching up with me, but I feel the need to eat before I sleep.' He began to move towards the door and then stopped with his hand on the handle. 'Can I bring you a Chinese? It's just as easy to get two as one?'

It wasn't an enthusiastic offer, just a polite sugges-tion if she happened to be hungry, and Leah realised that she was. Her stomach was empty and she was tired. A take-away would be the least hassle, just as long as Nathan Bonner intended taking his back to his own place.

'Yes, that would be nice, thank you,' she said quietly.

'Good,' he said, in the tone that a person uses when another has been guided by their wisdom. 'I'll be back shortly.'

The moment he'd gone Leah wished she'd refused his offer. She didn't want to be matey with the manage-ment, not when it came in such a disturbing package, and she decided that when he came back she would open the door, money in hand, and once she'd got the food wish him a speedy goodnight.

It didn't work out like that. Nathan Bonner ignored the money, waved a bottle under her nose, and glanc-ing past her shoulder said briskly, 'I think you'll find a couple of glasses in the cupboard,' and on that assumption he walked past her, slung his jacket across the back of a chair, and seated himself at the kitchen table.

As she placed the glasses on the table he said, 'Cork-screw?' and Leah thought irritably that it was probably the same tone he used when demanding a scalpel. But she supposed he *had* made the major contribution to the makeshift meal. He'd been for it. . .and paid for it.

They ate in silence, he with relish, and she, though just as hungry, with an uncomfortable wariness. The situation had been forced upon her, and eating with Mr Perfectionist at the end of a stressful day was the last thing she wanted.

When he'd finished Nathan Bonner walked across to the sofa and leaning his head back against the upholstery gave a satisfied sigh.

'That feels better,' he murmured drowsily. 'I was starving.'

Leah eyed him in dismay. She wanted him out, not making himself comfortable in her lounge. As soon as she'd cleared away he would have to go. Employer or not, this was her place now.

When she came in from the kitchen he was fast asleep, the disconcerting eyes hidden behind burnished lashes, the mouth that fascinated her so, softer in sleep, and she wondered wearily why the fates should throw a tempting morsel like Nathan Bonner in her path when she was on a man-free diet.

'Mr Bonner! Nathan!' she called, shaking his shoulder none too gently. 'You can't stay here. You have to go!'

There was no response. He was out for the count, and she stood looking down on him, fuming. The lights were on in his bungalow. If anyone wanted him they wouldn't know where to find him, and if anyone wanted her, such as the night staff in an emergency, they would think she'd lost no time in getting to know the boss.

However, the fact remained that Nathan Bonner wasn't the only one who was tired. She was exhausted, and if she didn't get some sleep would be fit for nothing in the morning, and on that thought she went into the bedroom, locking the door behind her, stepped out of her clothes, climbed into bed, and slept.

The alarm clock by her bed brought Leah into wakefulness at seven o'clock the next morning, and for the first few seconds she couldn't think where she was, then it all came flooding back, Barleyfields, the flat, her recumbent visitor.

That brought her up off the pillows, eyes wide and startled, mind jumping ahead to the embarrassment if anyone from below should find him in the flat at this hour. She slid out of bed and tiptoed to the door, and after unlocking it opened it a couple of inches. The sofa was unoccupied, the room empty; he'd gone. Some time during the night he must have awakened and returned to his own place, and to say she was relieved was putting it mildly.

At ten minutes to eight o'clock, Leah presented herself in the office in time to have a word with the night staff before they departed. This morning she felt more ready to take the reins in her capable young hands. She was neither damp or crumpled. Her deep blue uniform was uncreased and the small white cap lay crisply against the darkness of her hair. There was determination and purpose in the vivid blue eyes that dominated the creamy pallor of her face. Last night she'd felt tired and nervous, and having an overdose of the decisive Nathan Bonner hadn't helped, but today she was ready to get to know Barleyfields.

'All present and correct,' Anne Mirfield, the night sister, said with a tired smile. 'I've filled in the report book and you'll see that the only cause for concern at this precise moment is the condition of Helen Yorke in number seven. She's had bronchial problems ever since she came to us and tonight she seemed to be even more congested. She's on salbutamol and is propped up with plenty of pillows.'

'I'll get her GP to call in,' Leah said with an answering smile for the small grey-haired woman with kind eyes.

The night sister nodded her agreement and then said, 'How are you settling in, Leah?'

'I'm getting there,' she said with a wry smile. 'I suppose you'll have heard that I met my new boss while I was horizontal and decidedly damp?'

The other woman chuckled.

'Yes, I have. Barleyfields has just as good a grapevine as anywhere else. I wouldn't worry about it, though. It takes a lot to throw Nathan Bonner, and, flat on your back or upright, I'll bet he thought you were the most attractive thing he's seen in Barleyfields.'

Leah found herself laughing.

'I don't know about that. I got the impression that he values efficiency above all else, and it was in short supply when we met.'

Anne Mirfield shrugged.

'You're right up to a point. He doesn't suffer fools gladly, but when it comes to Barleyfields and his patients at the orthopaedic clinic he has all the patience in the world. Nathan Bonner is a very private person. You've probably heard that he lives alone in a bungalow in the grounds. As far as we know there is no woman in his life, not obviously anyway, though most of the staff are convinced there has been, and there are quite a few of them would be only too happy to rectify the omission were he to send out signals, but he doesn't, and that's it.'

There might have been more information forthcoming about her nocturnal visitor if the rest of the day staff hadn't converged on the office at that moment, and once they were there the conversation became general.

'Right, everyone,' Leah said after a few moments

of chatter. 'Anne is going to read the report for last night, so let's all tune in so that we know what's been happening to our patients during the hours we've been away from them, and then we can get the day under way.'

'We usually read the book for ourselves as we come in,' Annette Pryce said stiffly.

'Yes, well, that's all very well if we're short-staffed, or there is an emergency,' Leah agreed, 'but whenever possible I want all staff to be present at the reading of the report so that we are all equally aware of the state of those in our care.'

'It's wasting time,' Annette mumbled. 'Mr Bonner's always been happy enough with the way we do things.'

Leah's heart sank. The last thing she wanted was to be pulling rank on her first morning, but she'd already placated the disruptive redhead once and she didn't want it to become a habit.

'We're talking about a matter of minutes, that's all, Annette,' she said reasonably, 'and if Mr Bonner was happy before, I'm sure he'll be happier still to know that none of us can claim ignorance regarding what is happening inside Barleyfields.'

There was a murmur of agreement from the rest of the staff and Leah thought thankfully that there appeared to be only the one dissenter, unless the man who'd appeared in the doorway, and must have heard the discussion taking place, should be another.

It seemed on the face of it that he wasn't. Nathan Bonner strolled into the room with the same calm authority that he'd shown the previous day, and with a tight little smile said, 'Carry on, Sister. Don't let me interrupt.'

Leah straightened her back. The day was barely under way and he was here.

'I've finished, thank you, Mr Bonner. Just a small rearrangement, that's all,' and with a smile for the staff, 'I might have a few more changes to suggest, but we're not going to rush into them, and I can assure you that whatever they are, Barleyfields can only benefit from them. That's it for now, I think, so if you'd all like to start your duties, I'll be with you just as soon as I've phoned Mrs Yorke's GP.'

The exodus of the staff left the two of them alone, and trying to ignore his disconcerting brown gaze, Leah decided that now was as good a time as any to clarify a few things.

This morning her employer was wearing a dark suit with a crisp white shirt and a silk tie, a much more formal outfit than the designer jeans and cashmere sweater he'd worn the previous day, and Leah decided he must have an appointment, preferably a lengthy one.

'There are a some things I'd like to discuss with you if you can spare me a few moments of your time, Mr Bonner,' she said evenly.

He glanced at the watch on a lean brown wrist.

'I can spare you fifteen minutes, Sister, and by the way let's drop the Mr Bonner, eh? My name is Nathan, Nate to my friends, and when we're alone I shall use your Christian name as I do with the rest of the staff. Leah is a very old name. What made your parents choose it?' he asked abruptly.

She flushed, feeling suddenly faded and frumpish.

'It was my grandmother's name. . .and I like it.'

'Good. So do I, as a matter of fact, but we're digressing. Tell me, though, before we get down to business, did you sleep well behind your locked door?'

Her colour deepened even more, and this time it was with annoyance.

'You tried the door?' she questioned angrily.

The tight smile was there again on the fascinating mouth.

'No, of course not. I took it for granted that you

would lock it. After all, you didn't know me. I could have been the local rapist.'

Leah glared at him. They were digressing all right.

'It was merely a precaution,' she said stiffly. 'You don't look like a man who would pounce on an unsuspecting female. In fact, on short acquaintance I would expect it to be the other way round—that you'd let them know well in advance to give them time to dwell on the honour.'

He gave a dry chuckle, and his eyes glittered with what might have been amusement. . .or annoyance, but he didn't take her up on it.

'And what are these matters you wish to discuss with me?' he asked with a trace of impatience, as if it were she who'd been sidetracking.

He had perched himself on the corner of the desk and she went and sat behind it.

'I want to check with you whether I'm allowed to alter the running of the home without consulting you. Am I to be given a free hand or must I discuss it with you first?'

Leah had the satisfaction of seeing his face stretch in surprise. There was a moment's silence and then he said thoughtfully, 'I am presuming that any such alterations would be to the advantage of all concerned?'

'Of course.'

'You've been involved in geriatric care before?'

'Yes. I've worked on wards for the elderly and in a home similar to this.'

'All right. Go ahead, but bear in mind if I see any changes that I don't approve of you will hear about it in no uncertain terms.'

'Yes, of course,' she agreed, 'and now may I ask you something that concerns me personally?'

He was surveying her warily from beneath thick brows.

'What is it?'

Leah swallowed. She hoped that Celia Bonner wasn't being too optimistic when she'd said that her son wouldn't mind her having Katie sharing the flat.

'Is it all right if someone shares the flat with me? I did ask your mother and she didn't think you'd mind.'

His face had hardened.

'Who is it? Are you married?'

'No, I'm not. It's my young sister. She's in Canada at the moment, but she's very homesick, and as soon as I give the word she's coming back to live with me.'

He let out a long sighing breath, almost as if he'd been holding it back, and said, 'No problem. I'm all in favour of family life even though I've no experience of it. Send for her whenever you want. How old is she?'

Leah was beaming her relief.

'Thirteen. She used to be a pupil at Fairdene High School in the town centre, and they've agreed to take her back. She won't be any trouble, I promise.'

He was buttoning his jacket and checking the time, a clear indication that the meeting was over and Leah felt vaguely disappointed. He'd been extremely agreeable about Katie, surprisingly so. In fact, there'd been a brief rapport between them, but now it was clear that Nathan Bonner had other things on his mind.

'You'll have to tell me how she comes to be in Canada some time,' he said absently, and then, 'If anyone needs me I'll be at my rooms in Carlisle Street or at St Bernadette's. I feel I've been away too long and am eager to get back into harness.'

The night staff had given the patients their breakfast, and now Leah and her team were following on by assisting with the washing and dressing of those who were well enough to come down into the lounges, and, while they were being settled comfortably into their own special places, those who were less well were being washed and changed and helped back into bed, or settled into chairs by the windows of their room.

Leah had rung Helen Yorke's GP and asked for a visit, and had noted that he was a Dr Gordon Bell. The name struck a chord in her memory. There'd been a lad of that name in her class at school, a young swot who'd had visions of being the second Dr Kildare. Could it be he? She would find out soon enough, she reckoned.

When she'd gone to check on the ninety-year-old bronchitic, Leah had been concerned with the old lady's persistent coughing and breathlessness, knowing that, in the elderly, the borderline between severe bronchitis and pneumonia was soon crossed, and she'd felt that the sooner she saw her GP the better.

In the next room to Helen was Arthur Conway, a recent admission to Barleyfields. He'd been head-master at the local primary school and on his retirement had continued to be an active member of the community until the onset of Parkinson's Disease.

Leah had observed from his record that on admission he'd been depressed, without facial expression or motivation, and with tremors in his upper limbs. He had also become incontinent through lack of move-ment, and his distraught wife had felt she couldn't cope any longer.

But now he was much improved, and when Leah popped her head round the door Arthur was seated by the window reading a newspaper. A capsule of Madopar three times daily, and a similar dosage of Sinemet 110, were responsible for the change in him, along with regular physiotherapy.

'Hello,' he said. 'I haven't seen you before.'

'Yes, you have, Arthur,' she told him gently. 'You saw me yesterday. I'm the new sister.'

He shook his head.

'My memory's not what it used to be, but I'm a

lot better, you know. I must have been driving the wife crazy.'

'Yes, you are a lot better,' she told him. 'I've been looking at your record and you're doing very well.'

'Mr Bonner comes to see me, and he says I'm improving. I used to teach him when he was a little lad; a right handful he was. You wouldn't think it to see him today, would you?'

Oh, yes, I would, she thought.

When Leah went back downstairs Annette and Suzie were going round with the medication trolley, and Giles was divesting himself of a long shapeless black raincoat in the hall. In tight grey trousers with a mauve shirt, and his long blond hair tied back, he looked totally out of place and she started to laugh.

He swung round and eyed her enquiringly.

'This is the last place one would expect to find someone like you,' she gurgled.

He eyed her solemnly.

'My presence at Barleyfields does give it a certain ambience that was hitherto lacking,' he drawled.

'Maybe so,' Leah agreed, 'but I still find it strange.'

He had gone into the kitchen and was donning his white apron and chef's hat, and he called over his shoulder, 'I happen to be at Barleyfields because I was out of a job when I left catering college. At the time Nathan Bonner was treating me for a back injury. We got talking and he told me there was a job here for me if I wanted it and, of course, I was in no position to refuse. The pay's good, I have a free hand with the cooking so long as I keep to a nutritious well-balanced diet, and I don't start until ten o'clock, which gives me time to catch up on my beauty sleep.' He waved a hand around the gleaming kitchen. 'What more could I ask, unless it were that the delectable Suzie should seek to ravish me.'

The young care assistant was passing the door at that

instant escorting one of the patients to the bathroom. Gazing at him unabashed, Suzie said sweetly, 'The chances of that are about as remote as you getting your soufflé right.'

The doorbell broke into the amusing exchange of words between the two youngest members of the staff, and as the caller introduced himself as, 'Dr Bell to see Mrs Yorke,' Leah knew her surmise had been correct.

He still had the same shock of black hair he'd had all that time ago, and was just as long and lanky. The young swot had become a GP, and Leah wondered if Gordon Bell would recognise her.

'I'm Sister Morgan,' she said with one foot on the bottom stair. 'If you'd like to come this way, I'll take you to Mrs Yorke.'

'It's *Leah* Morgan, isn't it?' he said as he followed her up the stairs. 'We were in the same class.'

She smiled at him over her shoulder.

'Yes, we were, and you always wanted to be a doctor.'

'And here I am,' he declared. 'A respectable GP with a beautiful wife and small daughter.'

'So aren't you the lucky one?' she said with a small stab of envy.

They were in the old lady's room now and the conversation became professional. Gordon Bell's face was grave as he examined her.

'It's pneumonia, I'm afraid, Leah. See that she's kept upright with plenty of nourishing liquids, and I'm going to prescribe Vibramycin. If there is any further deterioration send for me, otherwise I'll see her tomorrow.'

The patient was listening with wide, anxious eyes, her breathing laboured, her hand on her fast-beating heart, and when she tried to speak, Leah stroked her forehead gently, but the words wouldn't come, she was too congested.

'Don't worry, Helen,' she told her. 'Doctor has prescribed something that will help you to breathe more easily, and I'll get one of the staff to come and sit with you.'

The old lady sank back against the pillows and nodded, relief in her eyes, and as they went back down the stairs Leah called to Annette, 'Will you send one of the care assistants to sit with Helen while I have the prescription made up?'

On the doorstep Gordon Bell said, 'Why don't you come to see us, Leah? I love showing off my family, and Gaynor, my wife, would like to meet you, I know. If you're married, bring your husband.'

'I'm not married,' she told him quietly, 'but my young sister is coming to live with me shortly and I'm going to be a bit tied up, I'm afraid.'

'OK,' he said breezily, 'but don't forget the invitation still stands, and bring the little sister with you.'

Annette Pryce was watching them, and when he'd gone she said sweetly, 'You seem to be on very good terms with Dr Bell.'

Leah gave her a cool stare. 'We were in the same class at school. He has just been telling me about his family.'

'Oh. So he's married?'

'Yes, it would appear so,' and then, because she objected to Annette's insinuations, 'What about you? Are you in a relationship?'

The RGN tossed her red curls. 'I'm divorced and waiting for Mr Right to come along.'

'Again?' Giles asked innocently from behind.

'The first time was a mistake,' she snapped, 'and haven't you got work to do?'

'I'm here to show Sister the lunchtime menu for her approval,' he drawled, 'and that is part of my job.'

Leah read it carefully.

'That sounds perfect,' she said with a smile. 'Let's

hope it tastes as good as it reads.'

'It will,' he promised. 'You don't think Nathan Bonner would have given me the job if I couldn't cook, do you? I had to do a trial run.'

She was curious. 'What do you mean?'

'I had to go round to his place and cook him a meal.'

'That sounds more like him. He doesn't strike me as the type to leave anything to chance.'

'He isn't. I'm surprised he took *you* on at face value, but then. . .what a face! Annette hasn't smiled once since you came,' he said with an impish grin.

'It was Mrs Bonner who interviewed me, and she had no qualms about offering me the post,' she reminded him.

'Yes, but Nathan does like to choose his own staff.'

'In that case, he should be around when problems arise,' she pointed out equably, and proceeded to where a relative of one of the patients was hovering by the door.

She was a middle-aged woman with a tired face and anxious brown eyes, and as Leah approached her smilingly, she said, 'I've come to see my aunt, Mabel Curtis. Is it all right if I go through? I know where to find her. She's always in the back lounge.'

'Yes, go ahead,' Leah said. 'I think I know who you mean, the lady who sits in the corner crocheting all the time. I'm new here and am just getting to know everyone.'

CHAPTER THREE

LEAH was happier than she'd been in a long time as she went up to the flat that night, firstly because the way was clear now for Katie to come back home, and secondly because it had been an interesting and fulfilling day, its happenings tucked away in her mind until such time as she wanted to go over them again.

Disturbingly, it was those few moments she'd spent alone with Nathan Bonner that dominated the day, and although he did come over as something of a bossy boots, if she was honest with herself she had to admit that he was the most memorable man she'd met in a long time.

A quicksilver mind was mirrored in the disconcerting eyes, and his direct approach indicated drive and purpose, a formidable combination, and yet he'd been completely reasonable about having Katie to live with her. Family life had his full support, he'd said, but he had no experience of it. It was a strange and rather sad thing to say.

She saw from her window that the lights were on in his bungalow and a bronze Jaguar stood outside. A car to match the man, she thought, a coppery powerful package. She'd had a feeling that he might make a second appearance in the late afternoon, but he didn't, and she'd decided that he'd been right about having a lot to catch up on at the hospital, or alternatively that maybe he *wasn't* going to be breathing down her neck all the time.

When she'd eaten, Leah phoned her father.

'You can book Katie's flight, Dad,' she told him. 'I've cleared it with my employer, and Fairview High are willing to take her back as a pupil.'

'All right. I'll see to it tomorrow and will phone you in the evening with the details,' he said reluctantly, still not prepared to admit he'd been wrong.

As she washed her few pots, Leah's thoughts returned to Barleyfields. There had been more time today to absorb the home and its functioning, along with the people in it, and one thing had soon become apparent. The focal point of the place, for residents and staff alike, was the corner where Mabel Curtis sat busily crocheting and offering her own brand of homespun wisdom to anyone who sought it.

She was a large woman with a cheerful smile and smooth rosy cheeks. A spinster, and well into her nineties, Mabel's mind was as clear and alert as that of a much younger person. Her only disability was a slight difficulty in walking and a reluctance to rectify the problem by moving about more;

The tired-eyed niece had told Leah, 'My aunt has been a very active woman. She's helped a lot of people in her time, and is very well thought of in the area where she lived. She has always lived with her brother, who's also unmarried and is a bit of a tyrant. Mabel had a slight stroke a year ago which affected her legs, and for the first time in her life she stood up to Rupert and told him she'd been looking after him long enough, and now it was her turn to be looked after, and so she came into Barleyfields. The old boy wasn't very pleased and makes a begrudging visit once a week, but Mabel is happy to be away from him, and as he seems to be managing reasonably well she can relax. She's been very good to me. That's why I come to see her when it's my day off from work. It's a bit of a rush as I've plenty to do with my sons and husband to look after, and he won't bring me in the evenings as he doesn't like visiting the sick.'

Leah had looked around her. All these elderlies were

in her care, and there must be a story behind each of them, as for instance with the lady in the tweed skirt and woollen jumper who'd eyed her haughtily on the day she'd come to be interviewed by Celia Bonner, and asked, 'And who might you be?'

Today she'd said snappily, 'Just watch your step, young woman. My nephew owns this place, and he listens to *me*.'

As Leah had eyed her doubtfully, young Suzie had laughed.

'It's true, Sister. She's Nathan's Auntie Myra, and never gets tired of telling us so. She's a bit of a pain, but he has lots of patience with her. I don't think he even knew she existed until she turned up one day demanding to be taken in. Mealtimes are the best! She drives Giles wild. She'll make a choice from the menu and then change her mind when the food is brought to her. It happens every time, and it would be understandable if she was failing mentally, but she isn't.'

'No, it would appear not,' Leah agreed, 'but you know Myra is far from well. You'll be aware that she's on steroids, and that her vision isn't good, as it's affected by her condition. She's suffering from temporal arteritis, a disease that affects the arteries branching from the external caratid artery, and if steroids aren't introduced at the onset of the illness it can prove very serious. The effect that it has on the retinal artery can cause blindness.' She gave the young care assistant her wide smile. 'So, you see, we have to allow for her little oddities.'

Today she had made sure that Charlie didn't take off for the farm at the top of the road, and consequently he'd been grumpy and awkward, but she'd promised him that if the people there were agreeable she would arrange for him to go at a certain time each day accompanied by a member of staff. The only snag with the arrangement was that it would have to be when someone could be spared, which mightn't coincide with the milking, and if that should be the case, then the only alternative would be to ask Nathan Bonner to get a cow, she thought wickedly.

Leah had left a message for Anne Mirfield and the night staff that she should be informed if Helen Yorke's condition should worsen, and that the only time she would be unavailable during the evening would be while shopping at the local supermarket.

An essential exercise, she told herself, as she slipped a white anorak over the jeans and patterned shirt she'd changed into. When Katie came she was intending to brush up on her cooking to make sure that her young sister was fed properly; no more eating out of tins.

It had been a day of spring sunshine, but now it was dark and chilly with a new moon hanging hammock-like in the sky. Wind whistled through the trees, and their branches made strange patterns where the light from the windows slanted on to the paths.

The bungalow was in darkness now, the smooth shape of the car no longer visible, and as Leah revved up her own little runabout she felt a stab of the loneliness that she'd fought ever since her break-up with Terry. It never surfaced in the daytime, but her evenings had become long and purposeless, and no doubt tonight would be the same, while her new employer was probably socialising somewhere. . .and if he was, so what? It was no business of hers.

She'd filled her shopping trolley and was moving towards the check-out when she saw him standing thoughtfully in front of a display of wines and continental cheeses, and it gave her a moment of pleasure to discover that Nathan Bonner was also occupied with the mundane.

Still wearing the formal suit, he looked less buoyant than he'd done earlier in the day. There was a tired crease across his brow and his vitality didn't seem so pronounced. Engrossed in what was an expensive display of food and drink, he hadn't seen her, and she could have left the store without encountering him, but on a perverse impulse she glided up behind him and said sweetly, 'There's five pence off Kraft cheese slices this week.'

He swung round to face her.

'Leah! I see you're here to remedy the Mother Hubbard situation like myself.'

She eyed her laden trolley.

'Yes, I've already done so,' and observing the display beside them with a wry smile, 'and all of it more basic than this.'

He laughed, and she had the feeling that laughter didn't come easily to him, but then she wasn't exactly a big chuckle herself these days. When her mother had been alive the house had been filled with laughter, but with her gone, and the discovery that Terry, who'd always had a laugh in him, was a thief, it had become something in short supply.

'I also have done my shopping,' he said. 'It's in the boot of the car. . .and I did take advantage of the cheese slices. I came back inside to have a look at the wines, in case I decide to entertain in the near future.'

'I see' she said flatly, attacked by a sudden Cinderella complex. She turned away, ready for off, but he stepped in front of her.

'Hold on a second, Leah. I want to talk to you.'

She eyed him warily.

'What about?'

He looked around him.

'Not in here, I think. Let's take the food home, and then perhaps you'd like to come round for a drink. I like to get to know my staff. I feel that it's important, and there hasn't been an opportunity so far.' There was amusement in his eyes. 'At our first meeting you

were involved in aqua sports, last night jet lag caught
up with me, and this morning in the office I was pushed
for time, In fact, it's been quite a day. I've been trying
to catch up on the backlog from six weeks' absence
with a list of private appointments as long as my arm,
and my clinics at St Bernadette's to bring up to date.
I also managed to find time to visit your predecessor.
Denise has made a mess of things, hasn't she?'

'It wasn't she who messed up her life,' Leah said
quietly. 'It was a reckless motorist.'

'Yes, there are far too many of them about,' he
agreed tartly, 'but from what I can gather she wasn't
entirely blameless. Most of those who end up in the
orthopaedic ward are accident victims one way or
another. It's all so stupid, and I can't stand stupidity.'

It sounded as if the man might have a short fuse,
she thought, and yet he'd been the essence of sweet
reasonableness when she'd asked him about Katie and
the changes she wanted to make in the routine of
the Home.

In the more powerful car he was back before her and
as Leah chugged up the drive he was waiting for her.

'We'll have that drink when you've unloaded,' he
said briefly, and she wondered what had happened to
their earlier bonhomie.

'Yes, if you like,' she agreed without enthusiasm. It
had seemed an attractive idea when he'd mentioned it
in the store, but something seemed to have put his
back up, and she didn't know if she wanted to spend
the evening going through the third degree about
Barleyfields, because it seemed as if his mood had
changed at the mention of Denise. Maybe he thought
herself a poor replacement and, if that was the case,
it wasn't fair. He had to allow her time to settle in. . .
to prove herself, because here she was, and here she
was going to stay, unless he threw her out bodily.

When Nathan opened the door to her she saw that

his good humour was restored, and she decided that it was just too bad as she was feeling unsociable now, and the visit was going to be just as short as she could make it.

He had changed into beige trousers and a tan silk shirt that matched the deep amber of his eyes and the thatch of burnished hair, and she could only admit that he was a very attractive man in anybody's book.

'Come in out of the beastly wind,' he said, taking her hand and drawing her into a large square hall with cream walls and a pale green carpet that was graced with a beautiful Chinese rug.

Curious about his home, Leah wanted to look around her, but although he'd released her hand the disconcerting eyes were on her and she felt the blood rush to her head. She took a deep breath. Nathan Bonner might be the most disturbing man she'd ever met, but it would take a Centurion tank to get through her defences after the Terry episode.

There was a half-smile on his mouth as if he guessed her thoughts, but if he did he made no comment, just ushered her towards the smell of tangy wood smoke and said chattily, 'These cold spring nights play havoc with the bedding plants, don't they?'

She stared at him.

'Er—yes, I suppose they do,' she agreed weakly, expecting something more heart-stopping than that.

'And so tell me about your day,' he said when he'd settled her in a chair beside a glowing log fire and poured her a drink.

'What do you want to know?' she asked carefully.

'Everything. What you think of Barleyfields. What it thinks of you.'

'I know what I think of Barleyfields,' she said immediately. 'It's excellent. What it thinks of me is another matter. Are you wanting to compare me with Denise?'

His mouth tightened. 'No. Why should I?'

She shrugged slim shoulders. 'I don't know, but the temperature seemed to drop after her name was mentioned.'

'Any drop in temperature was due to my anger at the mayhem the general public bring upon themselves. . . nothing else, I assure you. Regarding yourself, you are your own person. I don't expect you to be a clone of Denise. Obviously I will expect a first class job from you, just as my patients expect me to know what I'm doing, but apart from that it's all yours, Leah.'

'So you're not going to be breathing down my neck all the time?'

He gave a sardonic smile. 'I only breathe down the necks of those who need it. If you should turn out to be one of them, then, yes, you'll feel the draught.'

He bent to put another log on the fire.

'And now we've settled that, how about Helen Yorke? How is she?'

'Not at all well. I sent for her GP this morning and he confirmed that the bronchitis had turned to pneumonia.'

'What's he prescribed?'

'Vibramycin, and already she seems a little better, but she's quite poorly. I've told the night staff to call me if she worsens.'

He frowned. 'They're paid to cope. Don't make yourself at everyone's beck and call because you're living on the premises.'

She eyed him in surprise. One moment she was expecting castigation and the next he was concerning himself that she shouldn't be put upon.

She smiled.

'I don't mind. My social life isn't very frenetic, and when Katie comes I shall be in every evening unless we go somewhere together and, by the way, while we're on the subject of Barleyfields, I've told Charlie, our wanderer of yesterday, that if the folks at the farm are agreeable he can go each day in the company of a member of staff. It would make him very happy.'

He grimaced.

'Fine by me. For a horrible moment I thought you were going to suggest we keep cows.'

'It had crossed my mind,' she told him laughingly, 'but it was just an idea, and, talking about ideas, can I sound you out on this one?'

'Go ahead.'

'I'm afraid it mightn't go down too well with the staff, but I'm sure it would be better for the patients.'

'So what is it? Remember I did give you permission to alter anything you saw fit, without consulting me.'

'Even if it might mean employing more staff?'

'Ah! Perhaps you *had* better tell me.'

She twirled the stem of her wine glass in slim fingers.

'At the present time, the patients are given their breakfast by the night staff before they go off duty, which means, whether they're ready for it or not, breakfast has to be served and cleared away before eight o'clock.'

'Yes?'

'I feel it would be better if it were served by the day staff, as the patients could then have it later, giving them more time to gather their wits, and more time to eat it.'

'Mmm. I don't know, Leah,' he said thoughtfully. 'The day staff have the bigger workload and that would increase it. I suppose that's what you mean by more staff?'

'Yes, but not necessarily. I thought that if the night staff served just a cup of tea at say, seven o'clock to start the day, and then they, instead of the day staff, got the mobile ones up and dressed, and dealt with those confined to bed as well if there was time, it would balance the workload.'

'I *would* be prepared to take on one more member of staff if I thought it would benefit the patients, but it seems as if you've solved it, except for baths. Have you thought of that? The night staff can't be expected to find time for that.'

'It's too exhausting for the elderly to be bathed before breakfast and, of course, it's a weekly event rather than daily, unless there are incontinence problems,' Leah told him.

'Give it a try,' he advised briskly. 'If it creates any waves, refer them to me.'

Leah felt a small glow of satisfaction. He'd agreed, just as he had about Katie sharing the flat. The tyrant wasn't so tyrannical, after all.

'I'll implement it next week, I think,' she said. 'It will give everyone a little more time to get used to me.'

'Staff co-operating, are they?'

A tight face and auburn curls came into mind, but she pushed it away.

'Yes, fine. I'm very impressed with Giles. He's the most unlikely cook, but the food he serves up is excellent.'

The tawny eyes glinted.

'You see I know how to pick my staff.'

'You didn't choose me.'

The words were out before she'd thought about it, and Nathan eyed her consideringly. Leah had no idea what an enchanting picture she made in the soft glow of the lamps and the fire's flickering flames. The blue eyes behind dark curling lashes were challenging him, the beautiful face rosy from the warmth, and her body was the essence of sweet langour amongst the cushions of the chair.

'No, I didn't,' he agreed, 'but there's not much doubt that I would have done,' and as her spirits lifted, he brought them crashing down again. 'After all, you were the only applicant, and time was of the essence.'

She got to her feet, more annoyed with herself than with him. What was the matter with her? Why was she so obsessed with gaining his approval?

'If you'll excuse me, I have to get back,' she told him with chilly politeness. 'Thanks for the drink.'

'My pleasure,' he told her coolly. 'It's been a fruitful evening, I think. So far your suggested innovations are excellent. I feel that regular liaison between us would be a good idea.'

Whoa! Steady on! she thought, and then out loud, 'I'm taking it that you mean during working hours?' There was no way she wanted cosy little chats with the perfectionist every night.

'Possibly, but I do have a full work programme of my own. We'll see how it works out, but I don't foresee any problems. After all, we do almost live on each other's doorstep.'

Yes, and it's a bit too near, Leah thought, as she hurried down the path and in through the side door of Barleyfields, where stairs led to the flat. Too near, because the man who was her new employer had never been out of her mind since the moment she'd gazed up at him from the bathroom floor, and she didn't want that. Why couldn't he be a boring characterless individual, instead of disconcerting and desirable?

In the middle of the following morning, Social Services rang to ask if, subject to them going through the various channels, Barleyfields would be able to admit a patient badly affected by multiple sclerosis.

'We can at this moment in time,' Leah told them. 'Two short stay patients left yesterday, and so we have the accommodation available, but it would depend on how long your paperwork would take. The rooms could be filled by the time you're ready.'

'We'll speed it up,' she was told, 'if you'll hold a place for us. It's a fifty-five-year-old man we wish to place with you. His family have been caring for him, but it's got too much for them.'

'How long are we talking about,' she asked. 'A week?'

'Two at the outside,' the social worker told her.

'Yes, all right,' she agreed. 'We'll keep a place for him. I imagine it will be agreeable to Mr Bonner.'

'We've done this before and had no problems with him,' she was assured. 'Are we to take it that you're new?'

'Yes, it's my first week here.'

'Well, I don't think you need worry. We've always had a good relationship with Nathan Bonner. He and Barleyfields have been our lifeline on many occasions.'

Annette Pryce had been hovering while the conversation was taking place, ostensibly taking medication from the drugs cupboard, and when Leah put the phone down, she said, 'Nathan would have expected you to consult him first before leaving a room empty for goodness knows how long.'

That made her uneasy, but Leah wasn't going to let the conniving RGN see it. *Did* he prefer to deal with new admissions himself? She would soon find out, because at the first opportunity she would ask him.

It came sooner than she'd expected. He rang shortly afterwards from his consulting-rooms and wanted to know if a quantity of foodstuffs that his mother had ordered had been delivered.

'Not as yet,' she said with quickening heartbeat when she heard the decisive voice at the other end of the line. 'I have a note of it here on my desk, but they haven't shown up yet.'

'According to the invoice they were due to deliver this morning,' he said testily. 'It's someone we haven't dealt with before. There's never been anything wrong with our regular supplier. I don't know why she's done this. Would you check with Giles that we have adequate food stocks in case they don't deliver?'

'Yes, of course,' she said equably. 'I'll get on to them at once, and if there is any problem, I'll phone the regulars, if that's all right with you.'

'Certainly it is. I'm puzzled by the change of plan.' His tone was milder now. 'But knowing my mother, I suppose there'll be a good reason.'

'I would imagine so,' Leah agreed. 'She struck me as a very capable person. Shall I phone you back when I've dealt with it?'

'No. I know I can leave it with you. By the way, how is our pneumonia patient this morning?'

'A little better. She's had complan and fruit juice, and her breathing is improved. Her GP is coming to see her again some time today.'

'Good.'

There was a pause and she wondered what was coming next.

'I apologise for my irritability,' he said. 'The reason for it was certainly nothing to do with you. I've just had to witness a botch-up of a hip replacement that one of my junior colleagues has performed during my absence, and on top of that I felt that if my mother was going to bring in a new supplier she should at least have left a note explaining why. It's all very well you and I going shopping to fill our own bare cupboards, but I don't fancy doing a shop for Barleyfields!'

'Nor I,' she agreed, with a smile, and then said quickly before he'd time to ring off, 'May I ask you something?'

'Yes, but make it snappy, Leah. I have a patient due any second.'

'Social Services rang this morning to ask if we'd keep one of our vacant places for a multiple sclerosis patient. They're going through the motions, but it may be a week or longer before they're ready to place him. I

said it would be all right, that we'd hold the room,
but one of the staff said that you prefer to arrange
new admissions yourself. Have I done wrong?'

The tetchy tone was back, and this time it did
concern herself.

'No, of course you haven't. We've always had a good
relationship with Social Services. Hold the place, by
all means, and tell the person who was trying to tell
you how to do the job to mind their own business,
eh? Oh, and before we go our separate ways, I omitted
to mention last night, due to your rapid exit, that
Denise would love a visit from you whenever you find
the chance.' He gave a dry chuckle. 'You'll be able to
tell her that you weren't required to bow the knee
when we met, as you were in an even more lowly
position.'

It was quite obvious that he didn't mind being
described as a despot she thought, after he'd gone off
the line, and yet in a contradiction of terms, he'd been
extremely agreeable about everything she'd discussed
with him. Maybe that was his particular armour, as
was her own withdrawal from all personal contact with
the opposite sex. It was just a pity that Nathan Bonner
had such a kissable mouth and disturbing unreadable eyes.

When Leah went into the back lounge all the activity
was, as usual, in Mabel Curtis's corner. A young boy
from the fifth form at Fairdene High, who sometimes
came to help out with the chores, was being shown
how to crochet, and there was much laughter and clap-
ping as he came to the end of his first row.

According to Suzie, the lad was hoping to become
a male nurse and, as a keen member of the St John
Ambulance Brigade, he spent some of his spare time
at Barleyfields.

'He's a great lad,' Mabel said, when he'd gone
to help Giles serve lunch. 'I've missed never having

children of my own. These days not having a husband doesn't deter them. They don't bat an eyelid at becoming unmarried mothers. If that had happened to me, I'd have been sent to the workhouse.'

'You have your brother, though, don't you?' Leah said carefully, and Mabel's rosy face closed up.

'Yes, I have. It worries me that he's having to fend for himself as he's never had to do that before, but I couldn't go on any longer, I was too tired. I had to have a rest from him; he's very demanding.'

'You did the right thing,' Leah told her. 'You could have killed yourself from exhaustion, and then your brother would have no one. At least he can come to visit you here.'

'Yes, and he's fidgeting all the time he's here,' the old woman said with a tolerant laugh. 'If I ask him for any money, he doles it out so begrudgingly, you'd think we hadn't two ha'pennies for a penny.'

Leah had been glancing around her. There were twelve of them seated in the large lounge on the back that caught the morning sun and looked out over the lawns and beds of spring flowers. Comfortable sofas were scattered around for those who were more supple, and for the ones who required something easier to rise from there were high straight backed chairs. There were fresh flowers on the window-sills and in the corner was a grand piano.

Among those present were Mabel, Auntie Myra, a married couple called Jack and Jean who sat nervously holding hands all the time, Josh the old man she'd met when she came for the interview, and whose main interest in life was eating, and a restless Charlie, who, having been informed that the farm people didn't mind him going each day as long as he wasn't their responsibility, had his eyes glued to the clock awaiting departure time.

In the front lounge, which was more ornate but with

a less pleasant outlook, were the more seriously ill patients, some with catheters, some with frames, and one lady who'd lost a leg through diabetes, and Leah was reminded of her intention that the segregation should be discontinued. She called the two RGNs to her and told them, 'Commencing next week, I want you to mix the patients up more. Those who are failing mentally will do so more quickly without stimulation. They need to be among normal conversation, and to have the benefit of the brighter outlook that the back lounge has.'

'They won't like it,' Annette said.

'Who?'

'Those in the back lounge. They all have their own places. They won't want to move.'

Leah sighed. This one really did like to put the damper on everything she suggested.

'What do *you* think?' she asked the other girl.

'I think it's a good idea,' she said, 'but you *will* have some grumbling. The older they get, the more they become creatures of habit.'

'Hmm. Well, I think I know how to get round that problem,' Leah told them. 'Just do as I ask and I'll deal with the grumbles. OK?'

'All right,' Annette agreed grudgingly, 'but Nathan would want. . .'

Leah held up her hand to stop her.

'I'm running this place, Annette,' she said quietly, 'with his full approval, and so the gospel according to Nathan Bonner no longer applies. Do you understand?'

The swords were out now as far as Annette was concerned.

'That's what you think!' she spat. 'Just put a foot wrong, and then you'll see how much of his approval you've got!'

'That's not fair, Annette,' the other girl protested.

'Sister's right, and if she can get some of them to move, it will be better all round.'

'And more work for us,' she said, determined to have the last word.

Leah wasn't regretting putting Annette in her place, but she wished it hadn't been necessary, and she said in a milder tone, 'Let's give it a try, eh? If we all work together, it's bound to be sucessful.'

Any further acrimony was avoided by the arrival of Gordon to see his patient, and as they went up to Helen's room he said, 'I told Gaynor that I'd met an old school friend, and she'd love to meet you. She's from the far north of England and doesn't know many folks in this area.'

'I'll see what I can do.' she said with a smile. 'I'm hoping that my sister will be arriving some time later this week and once I've got her settled in we'll pop round.'

The old lady was propped up against the pillows and although her breathing was slightly improved, it was still heavy and laboured. After he'd sounded her chest and lungs, the young GP said, 'What about the sputum, Leah? What's it like?'

'Greenish yellow.'

'Mmm. That figures,' he said. 'She's a little better, but certainly not out of the woods yet. Keep on with the Vibramycin, and if she develops a temperature, aspirin or paracetamol should bring it down. It's a mildish dose at the moment, but if she worsens it will be a case of admission to hospital for oxygen therapy and artificial ventilation.'

'How do you get on with Bonner?' he asked as they went downstairs.

Leah gave him a quick sideways glance, wondering what was behind the question if anything.

'Fine,' she told him, and knew it to be the truth so far. 'He can be a bit intimidating, but he's efficient and caring, and although I haven't known him long, I feel that I can trust him.' The way she felt at the moment, she would rather have a man to trust than make love to.

And supposing you had the chance to do both, what then? a mischievous voice in her mind asked, but she was spared any soul searching as his next words claimed her full attention.

'Bonner's the top man in these parts when it comes to orthopaedics,' he was saying. 'His reputation is second to none, but, from what I've heard, his private life hasn't been as successful.'

Was it dismay that was making her heart beat faster? It certainly wasn't from the excitement born of curiosity. Whatever the reason, Leah didn't want to listen to tittle tattle about Nathan Bonner, and so with a vague, 'Really?' she opened the front door with all speed and ushered the chatty young doctor outside with the excuse, 'Ah! Here's the food delivery we've been expecting,' and surely enough, a white van with the words 'WHOLESALE FOOD SUPPLIES' printed on the side was coming up the drive.

As Giles was taking delivery of the goods and Leah was checking them off with the invoice that Celia had left, she saw Mary sidling into the ground floor bathroom which had been out of bounds since the overflow earlier in the week, and at the same moment Mabel came into view, moving along laboriously on her frame and heading for the same venue.

'What's wrong, Sister?' she asked, as Leah came hurrying towards her.

'It's Mary, our little water sprite,' she explained, 'in the bathroom again.'

When the offending Mary had been coaxed out, Leah turned to Mabel and said with a smile, 'I'll be coming to have a chat with you this afternoon.'

The elderly woman laughed.

'You might have to book an appointment.'

Leah joined in the laughter.

'You mean that the Barleyfields Advice Bureau is very busy?'

'I'm afraid so,' was the answer.

In the quietest part of the afternoon when most of those in the back lounge were dozing, Leah went to have a word with Mabel Curtis. As usual she was crocheting from remnants of wool that various staff and visitors had brought her, and when she saw Leah approaching her cheerful smile flashed out.

'How are you settling in?' she asked as the young Sister perched herself on a chair opposite.

'Fine, Mabel,' she said with an answering smile. 'I've come to ask a favour of you.'

'Oh?' The bright old eyes were fixed on her and Leah knew that this woman's mind was as clear and unclouded as any she'd ever come across. 'What is it, then?' she asked.

'I want some of those who always seem to sit in the front lounge to come in here,' she explained, 'and some of the folks out of here to move in there, so that we have a better balance. After all, this is the more pleasant room, and yet those who are the least well rarely come in here. I think they might be more motivated if they were mixed in with some of the more alert patients and seated in the brighter room.'

Mabel chuckled.

'You're right, of course, but these lot won't agree to it. I can promise you that.'

'Even if *you* were to make the first move?' Leah prompted gently.

'You think if I change rooms they'll follow?' she questioned thoughtfully.

'Yes, I do. You're a very popular person, Mabel. If they have to choose between keeping their own favour-

ite seats or losing your company, I've a good idea what
the choice will be.'

'Well, *I* certainly don't mind moving if you think it
will make it brighter for some of those who are far
from well,' the old lady said. 'But whether your plan
will work is another matter.'

Leah patted her smooth cheek gently.

'It *will* work, and thanks, Mabel. You're a
good soul.'

She rose to her feet and smoothed an imaginary
crease out of the skirt of her uniform.

'I'll let you know when I'm ready to try it, maybe
next week, eh?'

There was no bronze car outside the bungalow when
Leah came off duty, and she felt oddly deflated. When
the car was on view, it meant that the man wasn't far
away, and for someone who didn't want him hovering
all the time she was aware that she was a little bit too
interested in his movements.

Ever since the quickly curtailed conversation with
her old school chum, she had felt a small nagging
ache of disappointment. Nathan was decisive and
charismatic. It was hard to believe that he wasn't
successful in all aspects of his life. Maybe those very
characteristics were the problem, but who was she
to criticise?

She'd lived with a crook for months on end, in ignorance admittedly, but the fact remained that she had,
which made her less than lily-white.

Her father rang as she was finishing her meal and
the news was good.

'Katie will be arrivng at Manchester Airport early
Saturday morning,' he informed her. 'I'm presuming
that you don't work Saturdays, and thought it would
be more convenient for you to meet her if it wasn't a
working day.'

'That's correct. I don't work weekends,' she told him. 'That will be great! I'm longing to see her.'

'Yes, I suppose you are,' he agreed grudgingly, 'but she'd have settled eventually. It's a lot of fuss about nothing.'

It was clear that he was still peeved that his plans hadn't worked out, but she wasn't going to quarrel with him and so she changed the subject.

'How's Elise, Dad? *She's* happy over there, isn't she?'

'Sure. Happy as Larry,' he assured her breezily, and Leah thought that there was a world of difference between a mature woman with a new husband that she adored, settling into a strange country, and a young girl who'd recently lost her mother and left all her friends behind. There were times when her father was most insensitive.

It was a milder night than the previous one, and because she had the fidgets and couldn't settle to anything, Leah decided to visit Denise, and as St Bernadette's was only a short distance away she didn't use the car.

Every inch of St Bridget's Hospital was familiar to her, but the lay-out of St Bernadette's, its twin, was new ground, and she gazed around her with interest as she searched out the orthopaedic ward.

This was Nathan's world, she thought, where he no doubt ruled with the same authority as at Barleyfields, and if he was as good as Gordon Bell said he was, then why shouldn't he?

Denise was dejectedly flipping through a magazine as Leah approached the bed, but when she saw her visitor she cast it to one side.

'Leah!' she cried. 'It's good of you to come. I've felt really low all day.'

'I'm not surprised,' she said sympathetically. 'With

two arms and your leg in plaster you won't be getting many highs.'

The injured woman sighed.

'It's not that. Nathan isn't happy with the way my leg is healing. He's warned me that I may need a bone graft.'

'Oh, no! That's going to hold up your recovery,' Leah exclaimed.

Denise nodded bleakly.

'Bill will go spare when I tell him. He has the children to see to, and he's worried sick about me.' She managed to dredge up a smile. 'The only good thing is that Nathan's back. At least I know I'm getting the best care that's available. Talking about the great man himself, how are you getting on at Barleyfields?'

Leah smiled.

'Fine. In fact I love it.'

'And Nathan?'

'Like medicine. . .the first dose is a bit scary, but after that it becomes an acquired taste.'

'Just as long as you don't become addicted,' Denise cautioned with a smile.

'No likelihood,' Leah told her firmly. 'I'm just recovering from a very unpleasant episode with a member of the opposite sex, and it's left a very nasty taste in my mouth, but getting back to Nathan Bonner, I'd have expected a man as attractive as he to be already spoken for.'

As soon as she'd said it Leah felt ashamed. She'd avoided listening to Gordon Bell and now here she was trying to get Denise to talk about Nathan.

'There *was* a woman in his life, I believe, but it was a few years ago, before he came up north, before any of us at Barleyfields knew him. I don't know what went wrong, but it must have been pretty catastrophic as I don't think he's had a serious relationship since. Mind you, that doesn't mean to say he hasn't had women friends, far from it. After all, a man as dishy as he is unlikely to be ignored by the opposite sex.'

She turned her head on the pillow. 'And talk of the devil, he's just gone past.'

Leah swung round.

'Where?'

'He's just walked past the glass partition at the end of the ward, en route for his office, I imagine, and still in his greens.'

'You mean that he's only just come out of Theatre?' she said in surprise.

'It would appear so. It's been "joints" day today, and because of the extreme care taken to avoid infection while they're operating, he wouldn't leave the theatre until they're through. The air will have been specially filtered and he was in the full sterile regalia.'

'But why so late?' Leah asked.

'Must have had a very full list, I reckon, and he didn't get here until half-past two.'

'Yes, Nathan was at Carlisle Street this morning. He phoned the home from there.'

At that moment Denise's husband appeared with a huge bunch of daffodils crushed in his arm and anxiety written all over his face, and as Leah prepared to make a tactful exit, she thought that his worries were about to increase.

Making her way out of the ward she knew that she was going to seek Nathan out. If her pride needed an excuse it was to tell him that the foodstuffs had been delivered. It was inevitable that she would hold a post-mortem on her behaviour when she got home, but at this moment something was prodding her towards him and she didn't want to resist.

CHAPTER FOUR

HE WAS standing by the window still in theatre greens, looking out thoughtfully into the spring twilight, when she went into his office. She'd knocked lightly on the door and his invitation to enter had been brusque enough to make her have second thoughts, but she'd ignored them and gone in, and now Nathan was surveying her in some surprise.

'Leah! Where've *you* sprung from? But of course, you've been visiting Denise. Yes?'

'Yes, I have,' she echoed, 'but her husband arrived and so I left them. I imagine that they're both feeling pretty low at this moment. She's told me about the bone graft.'

He had looked tired and sombre when she went in, but his mood lightened a little.

'Yes, it's on the cards, I'm afraid. I'm going to remove part of the iliac crests as they're best for grafting, and then it will be back in plaster again with, hopefully, a fully usable limb in the end.'

He brushed his hand across his eyes and gave a weary sigh, and Leah found it strange to see him so low-key. He seemed tired and depressed, or maybe it was simply that he wasn't always high-powered, which was a comforting thought.

'Have you driven here?' he asked, breaking into her thoughts.

'No, I walked,' she told him with a wry smile. 'As if I haven't been on my feet long enough.'

'In that case, I'll give you a lift,' he offered. 'Apart from your aching feet, you shouldn't be on the streets alone at night.'

It was touching to be fussed over, but she wished he hadn't made it sound like a chore, that he had offered to give her a lift because he wanted her company, instead of appointing himself as chaperon.

They had only been driving a matter of minutes when Nathan pulled over in front of a restaurant and wine bar on one of the side roads leading to Barleyfields, and as she eyed him questioningly he said, 'I need to unwind. Do you fancy a drink?'

His face was only inches away in the darkness of the car. She could make out the full lower lip above the strong jawline, and the street lights were picking out the copper tones in the tousled brown hair, but she couldn't see the expression in his eyes. Right from the start, Leah had felt that Nathan's eyes were the mirrors of his mind.

She sensed something different about him tonight, a disquiet that was at variance with his usual cool authority. When they were seated beside the window in the wine bar with drinks in front of them, she said diffidently, 'You seem to be in low spirits, Nathan. Is everything all right?'

He was eyeing the ruby liquid in the glass morosely, swirling it round slowly, but at her question he lifted his head and sighed again.

'I didn't realise that I was making it so obvious,' he said with a twisted smile, 'or is it that you're a very discerning young woman?'

Leah gave an embarrassed laugh.

'I don't know. It's just that you seem. . .'

She paused. Why on earth had she started this discussion? His affairs were no concern of hers, but it seemed as if he wasn't of the same opinion. He was about to unburden himself.

'I saw a young boy this morning privately. Tests show that he has primary bone cancer of the leg.

Osteosarcoma to be precise, and it's almost certain that I'm going to have to amputate.'

'Oh, dear!' she breathed. 'But you'll have dealt with this kind of thing before, surely?'

He gave a bleak laugh.

'You mean what's happened to the impartiality that we learn to cultivate?'

'Well. . .yes.'

'I *have* seen it before, yes, although primary bone cancer isn't that common, and I've dealt with it in whatever way was required. In some instances, it's possible to just remove the bone and replace it with an artificial one, or do a graft, but there's always a chance of the cancer recurring, and in this instance I'm afraid to take that risk. Fortunately it hasn't spread to the lungs, or so I'm told, but we can't afford any delay, and I'm going to have to make a quick decision on what course of action to take.'

He drained his glass and placed it carefully on the table.

'This case is getting to me because he's a great lad, and I know the parents. The mother in particular is expecting me to pull a miracle out of the hat and save the leg.'

'That's hardly fair!' she expostulated quietly. 'Though I suppose it's complimentary that she has so high an opinion of you.'

'Not exactly,' he said with a bitter laugh. 'She thinks that *I* have a high opinion of my capabilities, and won't want to be seen as less than brilliant.'

Leah eyed him steadily.

'And is that so?'

'Of course it damn well isn't!' he said with an angry snort. 'I admit that whatever I tackle in life I have to do well. That's the way I am, a perfectionist, but it's not because I'm a vain blighter. It's because I can't stand loose ends or untidiness, and if because of that

I'm seen as a stroppy individual, it's just too bad. . . and I don't always get it right, you know, personally or professionally.'

'I'm aware that you haven't asked for my advice,' she said carefully, 'but if I may be allowed to give it, I'd say that the best way would be to forget what a smashing boy he is, forget that you know the parents, and ignore the pressure that the mother is putting on you. Don't be swayed by any of those things, just treat it as another case. It's the only way.'

'I can't, Leah,' he groaned, and it was in that moment she realised that what she'd thought to be disquiet was pure agony. 'I can't!' he repeated. 'He's my son!'

She stared at him aghast, blue eyes wide with horror.

'Nathan, that's awful!' she breathed. 'What a dreadful situation to be in. How can she. . .your. . .er. . . his mother, ask it of you? You can't operate on your own son! The strain would be horrendous.'

'My ex-wife doesn't see it like that,' he said flatly. 'If I *could* save Bobby's leg it won't be a case of earning her undying gratitude, even though she adores the boy. It will be seen as making up for my past deficiencies, but in any case I *have* to do it, Leah. I have the skills. I can't let someone else operate. He means too much to me.'

She nodded, but there was a question in her eyes, and as if compelled to answer it, he said in the same flat tone, 'I've just told you that I don't always get it right, haven't I? Well, I didn't get ten out of ten as a husband and father.' And he shrugged his shoulders wearily.

She reached across and impulsively took the strong hand lying loosely on the table into hers. At her touch, he looked up and the pain in his eyes didn't seem so bad.

'None of us is perfect, Nathan,' she said softly. '*I* had an affair with a crook, and lost my home and my self-esteem in the process, so you see how smart *I* am. Whatever happened in *your* past, your wife can't be entirely blameless. It's rare that anyone ever is in a marriage break-up.'

Leah was conscious that she was still holding his hand and she loosened her clasp, but instead of allowing her to withdraw it, Nathan's fingers tightened around hers, and he pulled her towards him across the table until their faces were almost touching.

'Did you know he was a crook?' he asked roughly.

'No, of course not! He was charming, well mannered, and quite dishonest. I sold my beautiful little cottage to keep him out of prison.'

'You must have loved him, then?'

Her face twisted as a vision of Terry pleading, whimpering that he couldn't face going to prison, that he would die if he was locked up, came into her mind, and she thought that compared to Nathan Bonner he was a useless, disgusting worm.

'I thought I did at first,' she said slowly, 'but in the end I loathed him, and yet I couldn't stand by and watch him go to prison.'

'You're a compassionate woman, Leah,' his voice deepened, 'and very beautiful. A rat like that didn't deserve you.'

He drew her even closer so that their breaths were mingling, and then he was kissing her, his lips gentle as they explored her parted mouth, and as Leah responded to him she felt an inevitability about it, a rightness that made her blood run warm, her heart leap, and the vows of non-involvement disappear.

If the kiss had started out as a gentle salute, it was that no longer. Passion flared between them, urgent, full of sweet desire, and yet only their lips and hands were touching. Then it wasn't even that. Nathan had removed his mouth from hers, released her hands, and was pushing her gently back into her chair. He got to his feet and stood looking down on her.

'I'm sorry, Leah,' he said gravely. '*I'm* the one who's taking advantage of you now, using you to combat my misery. Let's go, shall we?'

As she slid between the sheets, sleep was far away. It had been a strange, revealing sort of evening, and its revelations had been such that she wasn't going to forget them and drift off into a dreamless sleep. Her heart ached for the man who must mutilate his son to heal him, and she wondered what sort of a woman it was who would let antagonism intrude into such a situation.

Nathan had made it clear there was bad feeling between them, but he hadn't said why, and she wondered why a man of his calibre had stood by to let someone else bring up his son.

All of that had blown her mind, but it hadn't been everything, had it? Passion had flared between them for a few fleeting seconds, and yet it had been such that the memory of it would last a lifetime. But then he'd drawn back, saying he was using her to assuage his misery, and she'd wanted to tell him she understood, that she yearned to comfort him in any way she could, but there hadn't been the chance. He'd just led the way to the car, and kept grimly silent until they'd reached Barleyfields.

As they'd faced each other on the drive, Nathan had given her a long searching look, and then said tightly, 'Don't lose any sleep over me, Leah. I invariably cope, and I shall discuss it with another colleague before taking any action.'

Here was no cringing wimp, she thought, but a tough man having to make a tough decision, and her heart had gone out to him.

'What about the boy—er—Bobby?' she'd asked. 'Is he old enough to understand?'

'Yes, he's twelve, and all he knows at the moment is that the leg hurts like hell. If it has to be removed to get rid of the pain, I think he'll accept that.' He gave a grim smile. 'As long as we come up with a replacement sharpish. It's Maxine who's the problem. She's from Texas, and has been living in the States for years, until Dexter, the husband, bought an interest in a big UK concern, which meant them coming to live over here for a while.

'They've been in this country for six months and the first I heard of it was when I had a phone call early this morning to say they were coming to see me at Carslisle Street. Tests had been done in London, and she brought him to me as a last resort.'

He'd turned away.

'I'm bending your ear again, Leah. It won't do.' And before she could say anything further he'd bade her an abrupt farewell.

When she presented herself in the office the next morning with dark smudges beneath her eyes from a sleepless night, Leah thought ruefully that he'd told her not to lose any sleep over him, and that was exactly what she had done, but now, in the cold light of day, she was going to have to put Nathan out of her mind. Barleyfields was waiting, another busy day lay ahead, and as the report for the past night was read she fixed her mind firmly on the job.

The diary in the office said that some weeks previously it had been arranged that today the more mobile of the folks in the home were to be taken to the matinee performance of an amateur version of Old Time Music Hall. A coach had been booked for the occasion, and, once lunch was over, Leah and her staff were kept busy getting the excited theatregoers ready for their afternoon out.

Mabel Curtis, whose tranquillity seemed to desert her when there was any amount of walking involved, had opted out, and when the coach had departed and peace reigned once more, Leah found her busily crocheting as usual in her corner.

'Why didn't you go with them, Mabel?' she asked as she perched beside the old lady.

'Ever since I had my stroke I think my legs are going to give way when I stand up,' she said with a rueful smile at her own frailty. 'I'm fine in every other way, but when I try to walk I'm afraid.'

Leah patted her hand gently.

'I understand how you feel,' she said, 'but you must move about as much as you can. Your legs will get stronger the more you use them, and it will help to keep your weight down.'

Mabel chuckled.

'Does it really matter at my age, love? I've had a good life, even though I've never married. There's been my brother, lots of good friends, and we've been comfortably off. I shan't complain when my time comes. If I've one regret, it's not having children, but unmarried mothers ended up as lonely outcasts in my young days. There was no such thing as having the children without the father.'

Leah felt tears prick. This was a lovely woman, a motherly woman, who'd never been a mother. Old in years, but not in mind. She had yet to meet the demanding brother that Mabel had cared for so selflessly, and she wondered how he was coping.

It appeared that she was about to find out as Mabel was saying, 'One of the reasons I didn't go on the theatre trip is because it's Rupert's day for visiting, and he doesn't like his routine disturbed. Though I don't suppose he'd have jibbed at missing it for once.

He always makes a point of telling me how incon-
venient it is for him to get here. That's one of the
reasons why I didn't let him off the hook. In any case,
I look forward to seeing him, knowing that he'll only
be here for a short time, and I'm not at his beck and
call any longer.' The chuckle was there again. 'I bet
you think I'm a wicked old woman, Leah.'

'Nothing of the kind,' she replied. 'From the sound
of things, you've earned some time to yourself.'

'Yes, I have,' she agreed, 'even though I did have
to wait until I was a wobbly old geriatric.'

Leah laughed.

'You don't seem old to me, my dear.'

As the young sister got to her feet, Suzie was usher-
ing in an elderly man with receding peppery hair and
a face to match.

'Your brother to see you, Mabel,' she announced.

His clothes were expensive, but they'd seen better
days, and he had a white carnation in his buttonhole.

'This is Leah, our new sister-in-charge, Rupert,'
Mabel told him.

'Oh, aye,' he said brusquely, and with a brief nod
in her direction he lowered himself into the chair next
to his sister and said, 'It's chilly out there. Perhaps as
well I wasn't intending bowling this afternoon.'

Leah and Suzie exchanged amused glances. It was
one way of telling Mabel where he'd rather be.

'How are you managing?' she asked him. 'Are you
still getting Meals on Wheels?'

He gave a low grunt of disdain.

'Aye, but they're not up to what you used to put in
front of me. There's only two courses.'

Mabel sighed.

'What do you expect, Rupert? It's a nourishing hot
meal every day and that's something to be
thankful for.'

'I suppose so,' he admitted grudgingly.

'What about that one, eh?' Suzie said, as they left brother and sister together.

'He's a smart old guy,' Leah said with a smile, 'but he lacks his sister's charm.'

As she was walking along the hall towards the office, the front door opened and the man who'd never been out of her thoughts since last night was framed there. He wasn't alone. Nathan was assisting a tall, thin man with a fine head of thick grey hair up the step, and when he caught sight of her, he said, 'Ah! Leah! I've brought you a new patient,' and as he closed the door behind them, 'Let me introduce my very good friend, Thomas Whateley. He's been threatening to join us ever since we opened, and now he's finally decided to take the plunge.'

The old man looked tired and he was short of breath, but he gave her a warm smile and said quietly, 'Nice to meet you, my dear. It's true what Nathan says. I've been dithering for some time, but the old ticker has started playing me up and I know when I'm beaten.'

The door opened again behind them and a man in chauffeur's uniform came in carrying a suitcase and a tartan travelling rug. He held it out to the old man.

'I thought you might need this, sir,' he said respectfully.

'Ah, yes. Thank you, Harry,' Mr Whateley said. 'You can go now. I'll ring when I need you, and if any mail arrives that you think I need to see, bring it round, will you?'

'Yes, Mr Whateley,' he replied, and with a brief smile for Leah and Nathan Bonner, he departed.

'What about the rest of your clothes, Tom?' Nathan asked.

'My housekeeper's bringing them round tonight, and then she's going to shut up the house for the time being as *she*'s not getting any younger, either.'

'Tom is to have the suite, Leah,' Nathan said. 'It's

fortunate it's vacant just at this moment, and it will be ideal for him as most of the time he will want privacy.'

'Yes, of course,' she said, with a reassuring smile for the newcomer. 'We can go up now if you like, Mr Whateley.'

He nodded wearily.

'Yes, I think so. I *am* rather tired.'

They were about to ascend to where a small suite of rooms on the front of the house provided self-contained accommodation for the person who wanted privacy and just that little bit extra, when the lounge door opened and Rupert Curtis came out. When he saw the tall grey haired man he stopped in surprise.

'Why, it's Mr Whateley!' he exclaimed, his brusque manner falling off him like a cloak, the dour face breaking into a smile.

'Hello, Rupert,' he said. 'What are *you* doing here?'

'I'm visiting my sister. And you, sir? What's brought *you* to this place?'

Leah and Nathan stood to one side as the two men chatted, and she said quietly, 'And how does the world seem this morning, Nathan?'

He had been his usual self so far, brisk, managing, very much in charge, but now he gave a wintry smile and his eyes went over her face.

'If you mean from where *I'm* standing. . .very nice. Apart from that, the world is still turning on its axis, still full of painful problems. I'm sorry about last night.'

'Don't be,' she said quickly. 'I'm glad I was there for you. Have you given the matter any more thought?'

It was a stupid question, she knew that as soon as she had asked it. Nathan was hardly likely to have put the prospect of having to amputate his son's leg to the back of his mind, as his answer showed.

'I've thought of nothing else,' he said grimly. 'I intend to make my own diagnosis before I commit myself to anything, and I'm going to do as you advised. . .treat Bobby as if he were a patient. . .any patient. That's not going to be easy with Maxine expecting miracles in her usual high-handed way.'

'Any mother would want that. You can't blame her for feeling that way.'

'Yes, I suppose so,' he agreed, 'but my credit rating's not going to go up whatever I do. If I can't save Bobby's leg she'll never forgive me, and if I take any chances by not operating, which it isn't in my nature to do, she will never forgive me if the cancer should spread. However, I can't do anything until the results of *my* tests come through. When I get them, it will be decision time and there will have to be no delay. It seems that Bobby's had the symptoms for some time, but it's only since they came over here that they've manifested themselves to the extent of causing alarm.'

Thomas Whateley was beginning to look as if he was ready to be rescued from the now garrulous Rupert, and Nathan turned his attention to the two men.

'I feel that you need to rest, Tom,' he said. 'If this gentleman will excuse us we'll get you up to your room.' After Rupert Curtis had made his effusive goodbyes, they escorted Thomas to the lift and the suite awaiting him.

'Rupert Curtis used to work for me,' he said, as Leah settled him into a comfortable chair. 'He was in charge of the stores, hard-working, conscientious, and a confirmed bachelor, but there was never much pleasantness in him. I wasn't aware that he had a sister.'

Leah smiled.

'Mabel is a lovely woman, nothing like her brother. She's a very popular person here at Barleyfields.'

Nathan was checking the time.

'I have to be off, I'm afraid, Tom,' he said. 'I have

some people to see. I'll leave you in Leah's capable hands, and if there's anything at all that you want, just ask any of the staff.'

Thomas Whateley closed his eyes.

'Thanks for taking me in, Nathan. Yours is the only place I would consider.'

'It's our pleasure,' he assured him, and Leah thought that it *could* only be a pleasure looking after this charming old man.

She had rung for two of the staff to come up to settle him in, and as she and Nathan went downstairs together he said, 'What about your sister? She's due to arrive in a couple of days, isn't she?'

She clasped her hands excitedly.

'Yes! I can't wait to see her,' and her dazzling blue eyes were glowing at the thought.

He had his hand on the doorknob.

'Lucky little sister,' he said, and was gone, leaving her to wonder what *that* remark had meant.

Leah saw from the notes that Thomas Whateley had brought with him that his GP had been treating him with the diuretic Bendrofluazide, and point twenty-five milligrams of Digoxin twice daily to strengthen his heartbeat and to control any atrial fibrillation. Obviously the dosages would be continued while he was in Barleyfields, with staff checking for abnormal pulse rate before adminstering the Digoxin.

'That's the man who owns Whateley Engineering, the big works at the side of St Bernadette's,' young Suzie said, when she came down from his room after unpacking his clothes for him. 'He's got lots of money. Seems funny him coming to a small place like this.'

'Small is good,' Leah told her, '*and* he's a friend of Nathan Bonner.'

'Right, Sister, nuff said,' she observed with a grin, and then went bright red as Giles came out of the kitchen bearing a cream cake on a silver dish.

'I've saved it for you, Suzikins,' he said, with mock solemnity. 'Auntie Myra had her eye on it, but I managed to sidetrack her. She wouldn't go to the theatre in case she missed afternoon tea!'

'You're a tease,' Suzie said. 'You should have let her have it.'

'She'd already had two.'

Suzie laughed. 'Oh, well, in that case.'

Those were two nice youngsters, Leah thought, as she went to check on Helen Yorke, the pneumonia patient. In fact, all the staff were pleasant and hard-working with the exception of the red-headed self-styled leader of the Nathan Bonner Fan Club. The strange thing was that it seemed to be rather one-sided, as he certainly didn't go out of his way to talk to the disruptive Annette. However, the fact was that if *she* didn't put him out of her mind the fan club was going to have another member, and Annette wouldn't like that. With that thought in mind she applied herself grimly to the work on hand.

As Leah ate her evening meal later, she was satisfied with the state of affairs at Barleyfields. Helen Yorke was improving. When Leah had gone to see her she had been enjoying a bowl of nourishing soup, propped up with plenty of pillows. Her breathing was easier and it appeared that the Vibramycin was doing its job. Gordon Bell would be pleased when next he visited his patient.

In the room next to her, Arthur Conway was becoming more chirpy with each day, to the delight of his anxious little wife; and the new patient, Thomas Whateley, had been sleeping soundly when she had looked in on him.

When the multiple sclerosis patient was admitted through Social Services channels the home would be full, and as Leah absently bit into a crisp brown chip

she vowed to herself that the standard of care would
be such that neither the residents nor her high-powered
employer would have cause to complain. She liked the
job, the people she worked with, the patients, and as
a pair of speculative tawny eyes in a very attractive
face came to mind she admitted that she liked her
boss, too. . .quite a lot, in fact.

Her state of pleasant complacency was to be short-
lived. At half-past nine Anne Mirfield, the night sister,
came through on the internal phone to say that Mary,
the water fetishist, had fallen, and she feared that her
hip might be fractured.

'She's in a lot of pain and very agitated,' she said.
'I feel that I must go with her in the ambulance, but
if I do there'll be no one in charge.'

'I'll go with her,' Leah volunteered. 'Is the ambulance on its way?'

'Yes, she's lying where she fell. I thought it best not
to move her. We've put a blanket over her.'

'I'll be right down,' Leah assured her, and went to
pull the plug out of the bath of warm scented water
that she'd been about to step into.

There had been no activity at the bungalow during
the evening, and as the ambulance made its way along
the drive, Leah saw that it was still in darkness. It
had crossed her mind that the boy might be in
St Bernadette's, as it seemed unlikely that his mother
and stepfather would have taken him back to London
once the tests that Nathan had ordered had been done.
Maybe that was where he was. . .with his son, and she
thought that if Nathan had been denied the company of
his family before, he was making up for it now with
a vengeance, but in what tragic circumstances.

It was two o'clock in the morning when she came
out of the hospital. The old lady had been X-rayed,
and, as they had expected, her hip was fractured. Leah
had stayed with her until she was admitted to the ward

and then made her way outside to look for a taxi, reminding herself that if she didn't get to bed soon it would be time to go to meet Katie.

As she stepped on to the hospital forecourt, Nathan's bronze Jaguar was coming through the entrance and her eyes widened as she wondered what emergency was bringing him to St Bernadette's at this time of night. She shivered. Not the boy. . .please, not the boy. . .for his sake.

He must have seen her, for as she stood there, shoulders hunched against the night wind, he brought the car to a halt in front of her. As he lowered the window, she went across and asked anxiously. 'What's wrong? What's brought you here at this time?'

He wasn't looking very pleased.

'You!' he barked. 'Who else?'

'Me?' she echoed stupidly.

There was exasperation in his sigh.

'Yes, you. Get in, will you, Leah?'

She hesitated. The invitation was tempting, to get out of the cold night air and into a warm car, but it hadn't been made very graciously. He was acting as if she'd done something wrong, and with a sudden flash of anger she said, 'No, thanks. I'll walk.'

At that he leaned across, opened the door, and yanked her unceremoniously into the passenger seat, meeting her furious glare with equal fire.

'What do you mean, suggesting that you'll walk through the streets at this hour? Are you mad?'

She had had no intention of walking home, but she was blessed if she was going to tell him so in his present mood, and so instead, in a tone of sweet reasonableness, she said, 'You say that *I'm* the reason for you being here, but why? And why are you treating me as if I'm a nuisance? It may surprise you to know that I've been extremely upset and concerned on your behalf since last night.'

His hands slackened on the wheel and he turned his head to observe her, lips pursed, jaw set.

'I don't believe I'm hearing this!' he hissed angrily. 'I've come to pick you up! I was concerned that you were alone in the town at such a late hour. Right? And you are only a nuisance in as much as I arrived at Barleyfields well past midnight and went in to check with the night staff that Thomas had settled in all right, only to discover that Mary had injured herself, and when I asked who had accompanied her to hospital I was told that *you* had.'

'So?'

'So, you're employed from eight in the morning until five in the evening. I warned you that you might find yourself too accessible living on the premises, and whatever is said about me I don't expect my staff to work round the clock. Is that clear?'

'Yes,' she murmured, the fire gone out of her with the discovery that Nathan had been worried about her, even though it was only as her employer.

She leaned back and closed her eyes. She was desperately tired.

'It was my own fault that I got involved, you know,' she said drowsily. 'I'd told the night staff to send for me in an emergency, and as Anne had her finger on the pulse, it seemed more sensible that I should be the one to go with Mary.'

Leah knew that she was slurring her words. Sleep was washing over her and in the warmth of the car she was helpless to fight it off. He was eyeing her with amusement now. Making one last stand for her actions, she said, 'You might be my employer, but you don't own me, you know,' and then she was gone, limp and unresisting into oblivion.

She wasn't conscious of the car purring to a halt on the drive outside the home, but she was vaguely aware of being lifted out and swung up into strong arms that carried her effortlessly up the stairs and into the flat. When he laid her gently on to the bed her eyes flew open for a second, wide, vivid blue in a tired face, and he gave a low laugh.

'Don't panic,' he said. 'I'm not going to take advantage of you. This is where I depart.' He tapped the end of her nose lightly with his finger. 'Thanks for being concerned about us, Leah. I shall be making my decision over the weekend, and I can assure you that it will be the right one. . .for Bobby. After all, he's the only one who matters.'

He eased the duvet from under her and covered her with it.

'And as I've said. . .don't lose any sleep over *me*,' and with a brief wave of the hand he was gone.

When the alarm brought her into wakefulness at six o'clock the next morning, Leah's thoughts leapt back immediately to the moment when Nathan had taken her in his arms and carried her up to the flat. Her face burned. She had hardly been living up to her vows of being a 'Miss Efficiency Plus' at *that* moment. More like a limp lettuce as she had succumbed to sleep, but she had to admit that it had been very pleasant to be held against his chest with his strong heartbeat pounding against her breasts.

She stretched slender arms above her head and a slow smile spread over her face. Nathan kept telling her not to lose any sleep over him and this time her subconscious must have obeyed. It had been Katie that she had dreamt about, coming towards her across the airport complex, dressed in snowboots, a tartan lumber jacket, and a peaked cap with ear flaps. The dream had been so vivid that she would not have been surprised to see her leading a grizzly bear on a piece of string.

As she swung out of bed with joy inside her at the thought of the reunion ahead, there was a part of her that was remembering that the man who had turned out in the middle of the night to see her safely home would have nothing to rejoice about this morning.

CHAPTER FIVE

KATIE *had not* been dressed like somebody from the outback. She had been wearing jeans and a T-shirt with 'TORONTO BLUE JAYS' printed across the front, and when Leah had held her in her arms, Katie had felt thin and strange and precious all rolled into one.

'It's so lovely to have you back, Katie,' she said as the tearful youngster clung to her in the arrivals lounge. 'You've no idea how much I've missed you.'

'And I've missed you too, Leah,' Katie told her chokingly. 'It's been so cold, and the kids at school laughed at my accent. The apartment was nice, 'cos it was beside the lake, but it was near Yonge Street, and it's full of awful strip clubs and funny bookshops.'

Leah stroked her long blonde mane.

'Never mind, poppet, you're home, and *I'm* going to look after you now. We'll ring Dad as soon as we get to the flat to let him know that you've arrived safely, and then you can forget about Canada for a little while, eh? He and Elise have taken care of you all right, haven't they?'

Katie smiled.

'Oh, yes, but they *are* a bit soppy, always kissing and cuddling. Elise is nice, but she's not Mum, is she, Leah?'

'No, she isn't,' Leah agreed gently. 'But that's not her fault, I'm afraid.'

'Oooh! Isn't it big!' Katie exclaimed when she saw Barleyfields in the pale morning sunlight. 'And this is where you live?'

Leah smiled at her enthusiasm.

81

'Yes, in a small part of it. The flat's upstairs, and the man who owns the place lives in that smart bungalow over there. He has a son of a similar age to you.'

'Great!' Katie enthused. 'It will be nice to have someone of my own age around the place. Does he go to Fairdene High?'

'I'm afraid not. He lives in America most of the time, but he's over here at the moment.'

'I might meet him, then?'

Leah hesitated. She didn't want to discuss Nathan's private affairs with Katie. Maybe it would have been better if she had not mentioned Bobby.

'I doubt it, Katie. He's not very well at the moment,' she explained.

'Poor boy,' her young sister said, and Leah thought, Poor boy indeed. . .and poor Nathan. . .poor demanding Maxine and the American stepfather.

'Yes,' she agreed, 'but don't ask me what's wrong with him. It's none of our business.'

It was true, it wasn't, except for the fact that a short time ago she had witnessed the anguish of the man who was father and surgeon rolled into one, and such was the agony of his dilemma that she knew he was going to be in her thoughts constantly until the matter had resolved itself. If there was another reason for thinking of him—such as the memory of the surprising passion that had sparked between them briefly—she was not going to admit it.

After Katie had explored the flat they had a late breakfast. Though it was obvious that her sister was happy and excited to be back, it was also clear that she was very tired.

'I take it that you didn't sleep on the flight?' Leah asked.

'No, there was too much going on, and I wanted to watch the movie.'

'In that case, it's bed for a few hours,' she ordered,

'and then we'll decide how we're going to celebrate your coming home.'

Katie's eyes widened.

'That sounds interesting.'

Leah laughed.

'Yes, well, don't get too excited yet, as what *I* think we should do might not appeal to *you*. . . and vice versa.'

'I'd like to go round to see my friends from Fairdene tomorrow,' Katie said, 'so that it won't feel so strange on Monday.'

Leah glanced at her sharply.

'You're not worried about going back, are you?' Katie laughed. 'No, of course not. I know everyone, don't I? When I went to school in Toronto they were all strangers, and although some of the kids were all right, the others didn't want to know me.'

Leah's mouth tightened. Their father hadn't given any consideration to those sorts of problems. All he had been able to see was an exciting new life for them all, without taking into account that 'exciting' meant different things to different people.

Katie was asleep within seconds of getting into the other divan that graced the tasteful bedroom, snuggling down between oyster cotton sheets in one of Leah's nightgowns, as her unpacking had yet to be done. As Leah looked down on to the young face that looked thinner than when she had last seen it, her own loneliness didn't seem half so bad.

Leah went across to the dressing-table and picked up her mother's photograph, and as she studied the face that was so like her own they might have been taken for sisters, she whispered, 'I've got her back, Mum, and here she stays.'

In the late afternoon the phone rang and Leah's hand tightened on the receiver when she heard Nathan's voice at the other end.

'Your sister arrive safely?' he asked without preamble.

'Yes.' She couldn't keep the pleasure out of her voice. 'It's wonderful to have her back. She's asleep at the moment.'

'What about this evening?' he asked.

She frowned. 'I'm afraid I'm not with you.'

'Have you anything planned for this evening, or do you think she'll be too tired?'

'The answer to both questions is no. We haven't anything planned, and I don't think she would be too tired if we had.'

'Good,' he approved crisply. 'Then how would you both fancy coming with Bobby and me to see the new Spielberg film, *Jurassic Park*? He's very keen to see it, and I thought that the two youngsters would be company for each other.

'Yes,' she said dazedly. 'I'm sure Katie would love that, but where *is* Bobby? Is he with *you*?'

'He's staying with me tonight, yes. I've admitted him to Laurel House, the private patients' part of St Bernadette's, but as he's got a pretty grim week ahead of him I thought it would do no harm for him to come out for the night and I'd take him somewhere for a treat.'

'That's a lovely idea,' she said softly.

There was silence for a moment and then he said, 'I'm glad you approve. There's a showing at five-thirty, and I thought we'd go for a meal afterwards, if that's all right with you.'

'Yes, of course. Katie will be thrilled. I promised her we'd celebrate her homecoming, but I was a bit short on ideas.'

'And you?' he questioned. 'Does it appeal to *you* —an evening with the boss, and two youngsters?'

She was smiling, and if he had been able to see the brightness of it he would not have asked the question, but as it was, he was waiting for an answer. When it came, Leah knew it to be a watered down version of the truth.

'Of course it appeals to me,' she said casually, as if the thought of spending an evening with Nathan, his son and her darling Katie, was not the most pleasurable thought on earth.

'We'll meet you outside at five o'clock then?' he suggested.

'Yes, fine. I'll give Katie a little while longer and then I'll awaken her.'

'Super!' Katie cried, when she heard of the arrangements that had been made while she slept. 'It was on in Toronto, but I didn't get the chance to see it. . . and I'll meet the boy. What's his name?'

'Bobby.'

'And Mr Bonner. . .what's *he* like?'

Very memorable, would be a true answer, but that would undoubtedly make Katie curious, and so Leah murmured non-committally, 'Pleasant.' If that wasn't a lukewarm description of the driving force that was Nathan Bonner, she didn't know what was.

Nathan's son had the same thick brown hair as his father, and the gleaming white smile of American youth, but his eyes weren't the same, they were blue and apprehensive.

'He's more concerned about meeting Katie than his leg,' Nathan said wryly once introductions were over, and he and Leah were standing by as the two young people took stock of each other.

'Bobby's a fine boy,' she murmured. 'It's dreadful that this should happen to him.'

Nathan's face was grim.

'Yes, it is, but who knows better than we that life *is* dreadful sometimes? It can be cruel and unfair, and is certainly no respecter of persons.'

As they drove along the drive with Katie and Bobby in the back seat, the car park in front of the home was full.

'Saturday afternoon. . .peak visiting time,' Nathan commented, and then, 'Look, there's Thomas!' He stopped the car. 'I won't be a second. Just want to make sure he's all right,' and he sprinted across to where the old man was walking slowly through the gardens wearing an overcoat and scarf to protect him from the chill wind.

Nathan was back within seconds.

'Seems fine. Says he's settling in nicely. He's made himself known to Mabel. Apparently she was flabbergasted to discover that Rupert's old boss has moved into Barleyfields, and they've had a long chat.'

Leah smiled.

'She's just the right sort of company for him. Her mind is crystal-clear and her intelligence unimpaired with age.'

He nodded, and said, 'On the subject of our old ladies, I've been to see Mary this morning. The X-rays show a fractured femur as we expected. Fortunately it's across the neck, so I shall realign the bone ends and do a pin and plate repair. I would imagine that it was the fracture that caused the fall rather than the opposite. Mary is quite osteoporotic and might have swivelled round too quickly and the femur went with just that.'

'You're going to operate yourself?' she asked in surprise, glancing over her shoulder to where the atmosphere was slowly thawing in the back of the car. 'I would have thought you'd enough on your mind at present.'

His smile was tight.

'I have, and young Williams, my assistant, could operate on Mary. But when it's one of *my* elderlies, I like to treat them myself. The father in me can think of nothing but Bobby and his predicament, but the doctor part of me knows my work has to go on. I can't just drop everything. The results of the tests will be ready within hours and if my diagnosis agrees with the fellow in London, then. . .'

He didn't finish the sentence, but his sigh was enough.

'Where is Bobby's mother tonight,' she asked in a low voice. It was the question she had been wanting to ask ever since the phone call in the afternoon.

His mouth twisted.

'Gone back to the hotel to try to come to terms with what is happening. She's had two nasty shocks in the past twenty-four hours. The first was having to accept that I may not be able to bring a miracle out of the bag, and the second was Bobby insisting that he and I spend some time alone, hence our little outing.'

He was so tough, so matter-of-fact, and yet Leah could feel the hurt in him as if it were her own. She smiled. 'There's surely nothing wrong with that, for you both to be together for a while, especially as his young life is going to depend on you.'

'Yes, the dead-leg treating the "dead leg".'

'That was a tasteless remark,' she said with quiet scorn. 'It's the last term anyone would apply to you. What is it about Maxine that makes you feel like that?'

He shrugged. 'Old wounds, Leah.'

'They must be very deep, then, but I'm sure you're wrong. You have to be, or why would she bring Bobby to you? She'll want what's best for him and will have decided that you're it.'

He reached across and gave her hand a quick squeeze and at his touch her senses leapt again, but there was panic inside her. The more she got to know this man, the more all others became insignificant, and she didn't want that, did she? She hadn't intended it being like this. Her heart had been put on the shelf.

She gave him a quick sideways glance, and as her eyes took in the firm jawline, the strong yet sensuous mouth, and the thick waving bronze of his hair, Leah knew that this was no whingeing Terry, no light-fingered crook, but a man of strength and integrity. He might be volatile and demanding, but he was quick to understand the needs of others, while giving his own needs scant attention.

Her thoughts were interrupted by Katie's voice coming over clearly from the back seat of the car.

'And so what's the matter with you, Bobby?' she was asking. 'Leah said that you aren't well, but you look great to me.'

Nathan's eyes locked with hers as they waited for the boy's answer.

'Osteosarcoma,' he said with the same amount of nonchalance he might have used if it had been chicken-pox, and as Katie stared at him in perplexity, he went on, 'I've got a grotty bone in my leg, and if Dad can't make it better it'll have to come off.'

As her young sister nodded in calm understanding, he went on to give her a blow-by-blow account of what sort of replacement would be fitted if amputation should be necessary, and when he paused for breath, Katie asked, 'Shall I come to visit you?'

'Sure. I'd like that,' he said in his lazy Texan drawl, and as Nathan shook his head in amused disbelief at his son's prosaic acceptance of the disaster that was disrupting his young life, they drew up outside the cinema.

It wasn't the kind of film *she* would have chosen, and it didn't look as if it was Nathan's kind of entertainment either for every time she looked away from the screen, his eyes were on her, but their young companions were completely engrossed in it. When they came out Bobby said enthusiastically, 'Gee, Katie, that sure was funny when the brachiosaurus sneezed all over the small girl!'

She giggled, her eyes still full of the amazing spectacle they had just seen.

'Yes, it was, and wasn't it scary when Ellie felt the arm on her shoulder and it had been cut off.'

There was silence and she gave a small gasp of dismay.

'Oh! I'm sorry, Bobby. I didn't mean to remind you. . .'

He grinned, and in that moment Leah could see his father's strength and resilience in him.

'Hey, Katie, it doesn't bother me. Dad's promised I'll walk somehow or other, and as long as I can kick a ball. . .'

Leah was aware that she had been holding her breath, and as she exhaled, Nathan placed his arm around his son's sturdy shoulders and said smilingly, 'What a boy, eh, Leah? What a boy!'

'Yes, indeed,' she agreed, her eyes misting, and adding, without putting it into words, but being no less certain of the fact. . .and what a man!

As they walked towards the fast food restaurant in the cinema complex that Katie and Bobby had chosen, Nathan said, 'That elfin-faced kid sister of yours has got Bobby eating out of her hand. She's just the kind of company he needs at the moment.'

Leah was eyeing the place where they were to eat, and totally happy on the unexpected outing, she said with a smile, 'It looks as if eating out of hands is the order of the day in this establishment. Mine's a double cheeseburger and french fries.'

He smiled, but his eyes were sombre.

'Thank God for an uncomplicated woman,' he said.

She supposed it was a compliment, a rather abrupt one at that, but a compliment nevertheless. It didn't make her feel good, though. Uncomplicated often bordered on boring, and she couldn't see Nathan Bonner craving for the company of someone like that. What-

ever faults the difficult Maxine might have, 'boring'
did not sound like one of them, and she had a sudden
longing to meet the woman who had hurt him so much,
got under his skin to such an extent that she made
someone as capable and confident as he feel worthless.
The borderline between hate and love was often frail,
maybe that was how it was with them.

Leah brought her thoughts into line with an effort,
and told herself, what did it matter? He was her
employer, nothing else. The fact that he had kissed
her and she had responded utterly was just one of those
things. Lots of people were free with their caresses and
didn't mean anything by it.

'A penny for them?' he said, as he bit into his beef-
burger, his bright brown gaze holding hers.

Leah's colour rose. 'I was just moralising with
myself.'

'To what effect?'

'Reminding myself of the kind of life I've planned.'

'Let me guess.' Was that mockery in his eyes? 'A
husband with a nine-to-five job, solid, dependable, just
a little boring, a neat semi-detached to take the place
of the cottage you lost. . .and babies? Because you're
not going to let life punch you on the nose again.'

She glared at him.

'How very clever of you to read my mind so exactly.
You're right, life *isn't* going to catch me unawares
again, and I suppose that an uncomplicated woman
might be attracted to a man like that.' It was strange
how the word 'boring' had cropped up again. 'But
you've got part of it wrong. Men don't really come
into my scheme of things any more. I intend to be
very careful in future, as you yourself appear to be,
still being unattached after so long.'

As soon as she had spoken, Leah wanted to bite the
words back. Whatever had possessed her to let him
see that he interested her to such an extent?

He was assessing her over the top of the burger.

'I see. So you're of the opinion that we're both suffering from the "once bitten" complex. Well, it's certainly true in my case, although I can appreciate a beautiful woman as well as any man, and I don't make a point of avoiding them. You're one yourself, Leah Morgan, but I can't quite make you out. *You* fell in love with a con-man, and *I* married a rich American, and both relationships were a catastrophe, and now we're wary—at least *you* are,' his voice hardened, 'and if you're trying to tell me something. . .consider it told.'

Dismay hit her in a demoralising tide. Whatever had possessed her to bring the subject up, risking the snub that she had just received, and why on earth had she not told him the truth, that men had been out of her life only until the day she met *him*.

'Bobby isn't feeling well,' Katie called from the table they were sharing nearby, and immediately Nathan and Leah were on their feet.

'What is it, son?' he asked quickly, his keen eyes raking the boy's face.

'It's just the pain,' Bobby said. 'It's making me feel sick.'

'Let's get you home then,' Nathan said briskly, and to Leah, 'Do you want to hang on here, or come with us?'

'We'll come with you, of course,' she replied, and Katie, who had been observing her new-found friend anxiously, nodded in emphatic agreement.

'Is it *all* the leg that's painful?' Leah asked in a low voice as they drove back to Barleyfields.

'It's centred mostly just below the knee,' Nathan explained. 'I can keep the pain controlled up to a point, but sometimes it gets too much for him. If I *do* have to amputate, it will be to the nearest proximal point, which in Bobby's case will be just *above* the knee.'

'So the prosthesis would need to have two joints. . . the knee and the ankle?'

He nodded grimly, and glanced over his shoulder to where Katie was trying to take Bobby's mind off the pain by talking about the film.

'The tests carried out in London show there are no secondary lesions in the lungs so far, for which we all offered up a prayer of thanks, but I still want to have my own tests done. Bobby has had bone scans and magnetic resonance imaging at my request. It's very expensive and not always available, but fortunately, with regard to our son, Maxine and I can well afford it, and I would hope that it will be generally available to all patients soon.'

'What exactly does it entail?' she asked.

'The patient lies inside a huge hollow cylinder-shaped magnet, and during the process the hydrogen nuclei are knocked out of line by strong radio waves, which causes them to produce a detectable radio signal as they fall back into position. Coils in the machine pick up the signals and they're changed into a three-dimensional image based on the power of the signal. The images it produces are quite similar to those from a CT scan, but with magnetic resonance imaging there's a better contrast between what is normal and what is abnormal tissue and, of course, the beauty of it is that there are no risks. The results from it, along with bone X-rays and biopsies, will be available very soon, and then I shall make my decision.

'Basically I have three choices. I can remove the diseased bone and replace it with an artificial one, or remove it and attempt a bone graft, or. . .amputate. In the first two instances there is always the chance that we won't have caught all the cancer, which could endanger Bobby's life even more than at present. The third choice, which is, of course, the most horrific, is the safest. If the limb is removed and the operation followed by a course of chemotherapy, there is a strong prospect of complete recovery, but with an artificial leg in Bobby's case.'

'To what extent does your wife understand the possibility of *that* having to be the choice?' Leah asked carefully.

'My ex-wife,' he corrected stonily, 'isn't able to cope with that eventuality at present. Dexter, her husband, is trying to talk her through it, but she's convinced that I'm going to save the leg. She feels that as I'm personally involved, I'll perform better.'

'That's insulting,' Leah said with quiet anger. 'It's implying that you would do less than your best if you weren't involved.'

He shrugged.

'I don't suppose she means it exactly like that. With Maxine, it's more a case of giving me the chance to redeem myself, as I've explained before. Though God knows what I did wrong, unless it was bringing a rich girl all the way from Daddy's ranch in Texas and expecting her to live in a mediocre bedsit in England while I ran myself ragged on the wards as a junior doctor. *I* didn't want it that way. It was her choice. I'd have preferred her to stay in Texas until I was established and could support her in the way she was used to. I was ambitious, not afraid of hard work, and knew I would get to the top sooner or later. She could have stayed with her parents and we'd have commuted whenever possible. Maybe not the most satisfactory of arrangements, but it would have worked if she'd given it a chance. However, Maxine wouldn't agree to that. She wanted us to be together in our little love-nest.'

'And?' she asked softly.

'The novelty wore off faster than the speed of light as she became pregnant almost immediately and I was hardly ever there. In the end, she went back to Texas on what was supposed to be a holiday. . .and never came back.'

'And you accepted it, just like that?'

'No, I didn't. I went over there like a tornado, demanding that my wife and child return to me, but Pops had other ideas and so did his daughter. First of all, they wanted me to transfer to an American hospital, which I would have considered if it hadn't been in the form of a command. When that didn't work, he offered to buy us a big spread over here. I refused that, too. Maxine knew what she was letting herself in for when she married me, and as far as I was concerned, if she stuck with me it would be a matter of waiting until *I* could provide her with a better lifestyle, not a situation where we were living out of the old man's pocket. In the end they offered to buy me off if I would divorce her, and that didn't work either. Yet I was the one who came away defeated. I lost my wife and child. All right, I had access to Bobby, but at that time my salary didn't allow frequent trips to America, and when I *did* go, Maxine created such a rumpus that Bobby became upset and insecure. In the end, I gave her the divorce, and did the hardest thing I've ever had to do in my life, that is, until now. I cut myself off from my son, for his sake, not mine.'

Leah was silent. She could imagine the rich American girl falling in love with the implacable force that was Nathan Bonner, and being so besotted with the charismatic medical student that she could think of nothing else, and then coming down to earth with a bump.

The high roof of Barleyfields was in view, in seconds they would be back inside their respective abodes, but he had one last thing to say. 'As someone who has acquired a jaundiced view of the opposite sex, what would *you* have done in her place?'

She eyed him consideringly, taking in every detail

of the face that seemed to be continually in her mind, and then she said slowly, 'I would have thought long and hard about it, and if I'd come to the conclusion that my love for you was just as strong as when we were first married, I would have stayed, as I'd have known I couldn't bear to lose you, that nothing could keep us apart. On the other hand, if I had decided that I'd fallen out of love with you. . .bearing in mind that this is all hypothetical. . .'

'Yes,' he agreed impatiently as the car turned into the drive, 'and?'

'Because I was a pampered little rich girl who couldn't cope, I would have straightened my shoulders, tightened my belt, and been grateful for a husband who loved me and was a man of principle.'

'Hmmm,' he murmured. 'Pity *you* weren't around at the time.'

'What? In my gymslip and blazer?' she asked with a smile that concealed the confusion that the casual words had created in her.

He gave his raffish grin.

'Point taken, Sister, but do remember that older men *are* the most interesting, though I'm forgetting *you're* not interested in any of us, are you?'

'Correct,' she replied firmly, and knew it to be a lie.

They separated outside the bungalow with Bobby leaning heavily on his father's arm, and Katie telling the boy earnestly that the pain would soon be gone, one way or another, and for a moment his earlier breezy cheerfulness was back.

Leah and Nathan exchanged glances above their heads.

'I'm a person who rarely asks favours of anyone,' he said in a low voice, 'but in this instance, may I, Leah?'

She felt her face go warm.

'Yes, of course. What is it?'

'Pray for us.'

Her eyes filled with tears. At that moment there was no bounce in him, no authority, just a sombre calm that was more upsetting than any display of emotion.

'There's no need to ask that of me,' she whispered. 'I would do so in any case. I know that you'll make the right decision, and from what I've been told, Bobby couldn't be in better hands. Do please let me know what you decide as you'll both be in my thoughts.'

He looked surprised.

'Well, yes, of course, that goes without saying. I'll be in touch once I know what I'm going to do.' And on that promise he took Bobby's arm and led him inside.

GET 4 BOOKS
A CUDDLY TEDDY
AND A MYSTERY GIFT

FREE

Return this card, and we'll send you 4 Mills & Boon romances, absolutely FREE! We'll even pay the postage and packing for you!

We're making you this offer to introduce to you the benefits of Mills & Boon Reader Service: FREE home delivery of brand-new Mills & Boon romances, at least a month before they're available in the shops, FREE gifts and a monthly Newsletter packed with special offers and information.

Accepting these FREE books places you under no obligation to buy, you may cancel at any time, even after receiving just your free shipment.

Yes, please send me 4 free Mills & Boon romances, a cuddly teddy and a mystery gift as explained above. Please also reserve a Reader Service subscription for me. If I decide to subscribe, I shall receive 6 superb new titles every month for just £11.40 postage and packing free. If I decide not to subscribe I shall write to you within 10 days. The free books and gifts will be mine to keep in any case. I understand that I am under no obligation whatsoever. I may cancel or suspend my subscription at any time simply by writing to you.

Ms/Mrs/Miss/Mr _____ 10A4R

Address _____

_____

_____ Postcode_____

Signature_____
I am over 18 years of age.

Get 4 books
a cuddly teddy and
mystery gift FREE!

SEE BACK OF CARD FOR DETAILS

Mills & Boon Reader Service,
FREEPOST
P.O. Box 236
Croydon
CR9 9EL

No
stamp
needed

CHAPTER SIX

ON SUNDAY morning Leah awoke to find Katie beside
the bed with a laden breakfast tray and, as she blinked
in surprise, her young sister pointed to a single daffodil
in a small glass vase, drooping in golden splendour
beside the toast and marmalade.

'Freshly picked with the dew still on it,' she said,
with a happy giggle.

Its recipient groaned.

'Dew! Why, what time is it?'

'Half-past six.'

'Katie!' she protested. 'It's Sunday morning!'

The young waitress placed the tray on the bedside
table and snuggled in beside her.

'Yes, I know. The birds awoke me, and after that
I couldn't get back to sleep. It's so exciting to be home,
Leah. How soon do you think I could go to see my
friends? I can't wait to catch up on all the news.'

Leah laughed sleepily.

'Well, certainly not yet. I'd wait an hour or two at
least. Most families get up later on Sundays.' She raised
herself up on the pillows. 'And as you've gone to all
this trouble, let's forget your social arrangements for
a moment. . .and eat.'

It seemed strange, the two of them munching away
in the quiet flat, while down below the night staff would
be giving the residents of Barleyfields their morning
tea and gently moving them towards another day. She
wondered how Mary was coping in St Bernadette's, if
Helen Yorke was still improving, and how Nathan's
friend Thomas Whateley was this morning.

When they had finished Katie picked up the tray

and Leah said with a smile, 'I presume the daffodil is courtesy of Barleyfields?'

She nodded.

'Mmm. As I was picking it an old lady knocked on the window and told me I was trespassing.'

'That sounds like Auntie Myra,' Leah said. 'And what did *you* say?'

'I told her that I lived here.'

Leah's smile flashed out again.

'Only just.'

Katie's mind was already on another train of thought.

'I saw Bobby and his father drive off while I was in the garden.'

'*So* early!' she exclaimed in surprise.

'Yes, they waved as they went past. Do you think he would be taking him back to hospital?'

'I would imagine so,' she said sombrely.

When Mabel Curtis came downstairs on Monday morning, at a sign from Leah she turned her Zimmer frame in the direction of the front lounge, and was watched in some amazement by those who usually sat beside her.

'What are you doing in here?' Auntie Myra wanted to know as Mabel settled herself into one of the chairs and took out her crocheting.

'I'm having a change,' she told her cheerfully. 'I barely know some of the folks who sit in here, which seems all wrong when we're living together.'

Leah was hovering in the doorway and Mabel gave a sly wink.

'Why don't you come and join me?' she suggested to the surprised Myra. 'Maybe Jack and Jean would like to come in here too?'

Myra gave an indignant snort.

'Those two! They'd be frightened of moving in case

somebody commandeered the settee. They're like Siamese twins. The only thing they don't do together is go to the toilet.'

'They *are* very dependent on each other, it's true,' Mabel agreed, 'but they're a sweet gentle couple who are feeling rather timid and insecure, and it's rare to see such devotion these days. Why not go and ask them, eh, Myra?'

'All right,' she said grudgingly, and as she toddled off, Leah gave the chuckling Mabel the thumbs-up sign.

Thomas Whateley was seated beside the window of his small lounge reading the *Telegraph* when she went to check on him. He was smartly dressed in grey trousers, white shirt and a subdued tie, with a dark blue cardigan over them that highlighted his stylishly cut grey hair. He would have been a very presentable old man if it hadn't been for his extreme thinness.

Leah saw that his breakfast tray had barely been touched and she eyed him anxiously. Most elderly people, unless quite ill, were good eaters for two reasons, the first being their determination to survive, and the second because mealtimes were something to look forward to when life hadn't as much to offer as it once had. If Thomas Whateley wasn't eating, it could account for his lack of weight, and there was usually a good reason for loss of appetite.

'Are you not hungry, Thomas?' she asked, pointing to the tray.

He shook his head.

'No, Sister. I had a bad dose of bronchitis a couple of months ago and what little appetite I had before it seems to have gone.' He cleared his throat and she could hear some congestion still there. 'My GP tells me that I've got ischaemic heart disease. I've been on vasodilator drugs, and he's warned me that I might require balloon angioplasty or a bypass.' He gave a tired smile. 'If it does come to that and I have a choice in the matter, I think I'll plump for the bypass. I'm not too sure that I fancy this ballooning business.'

'It *can* be very successful,' she assured him. 'It opens up the narrowed arteries and lets the blood flow through more easily, but let's not worry about that at the moment, eh? The eventuality may never arise, and in the meantime I'm going to see if we can tempt you to eat a little more. Complan and plenty of fresh fruit should help to bring your appetite back, and perhaps some concentrated vitamins to make up for what you're missing in your diet. There is a Swiss preparation that is excellent. It has all the vitamins anyone could possibly need in the capsule, and although it's quite expensive, the results are well worth the cost. I'll speak to Nathan about it.'

He held up a thin hand.

'Don't bother Nathan about it, my dear. He's a busy man. If you think the preparation will do me good then get it. The cost is of no consequence. I can't take my money with me.'

'That's true,' she agreed with a smile, and then, because she seemed unable to control her interest in the man he'd just mentioned, she asked, 'How long have you known Nathan, Mr Whateley?'

'A few years. I met him when he was treating my wife for severe neck pain and numbness of the hands. It turned out to be osteoarthritis and she was a patient of his for quite some time, as it's not the kind of thing that goes away. We'd never had family, and as I got to know him better Nathan was like the son I'd never had. I admire everything about him, especially his drive and energy. . .and his complete integrity.'

'He doesn't rate himself very high when he talks about his marriage,' she said.

He stared at her in surprise.

'He's discussed it with you?'

'Er. . .yes,' she admitted hesitantly.

'That's amazing. I've never known him do that before, not even with Maisie and me. I've put two and two together, of course, and come to the conclusion that it was most likely a clash of two very strong personalities that caused it to break up.'

And *he* seems to have come off worst in the skirmish, Leah was thinking as Helen Yorke's bell started to ring.

She found the old lady on the floor with the bell rope clutched in her hand. Helen was lying motionless, hunched on her left side, and as Leah ran to her, she saw that her lips were blue and her eyes glazed. She felt her neck and laid her ear to her chest to check for a heartbeat, but she knew there wasn't going to be any. She was dead. Leah eased the buzzer out of her hand to ring for help but it didn't work, and when she looked up the reason was obvious, Helen had wrenched it out of the socket with the force of her fall.

Gordon Bell was sent for and pronounced life extinct, and as he and Leah stood looking down on the peaceful old lady he said, 'Her heart hasn't been good for some time, and the constant coughing and breathing difficulties will have taken their toll. It was a massive heart attack, swift and final.'

She nodded gravely. 'Yes, and she was doing so well. I thought she was going to fight off the pneumonia.'

He sighed. 'It's enough to cope with at any time, but when the patient is in the nineties. . .'

As he signed the death certificate, Leah kept to general topics. For some reason she didn't want to give him the opportunity of discussing Nathan again. It was crazy, because only a short time earlier she had been only too willing to discuss him with Thomas Whateley, but then the old man was Nathan's friend, while Gordon Bell merely knew him as a member of the same profession.

When he had gone, she went into the kitchen and made coffee, feeling low and depressed. Helen's death had saddened her, and at the back of her mind all the time were Nathan and Bobby, and the dreadful time that lay ahead of them. He'd promised to be in touch and until she heard from him she was going to be worried and restless.

It appeared that she was the only one aware of his predicament, as no mention of his son's illness had been made by any of the staff, which was not surprising if none of them knew about his domestic circumstances. Thomas Whateley had made no reference to it either and, inexplicably, it gave her a warm feeling inside to know that he had confided in *her* alone.

For the rest of the day there was a feeling of gentle regret inside Barleyfields. Helen Yorke hadn't mixed much with the other residents as she had been unwell ever since being admitted, and so most of them were unaware of her demise, but there was sadness among the staff and Suzie described their feelings exactly.

'When you're with them every day, week after week, coping with their ups and downs, washing them, dressing them, they become like family,' she said with a depth of feeling that surprised Leah. 'Even Giles filled up when he heard that she'd gone.'

Her records in the office showed that a nephew in Somerset was the only relative, and after Leah had phoned to tell him of his aunt's death, she tried to get hold of Nathan. Whatever was going on in his life at the moment he would have to be informed, as he had stressed that his other commitments must not be ignored because of Bobby's illness, but when she rang his rooms at Carlisle Street and St Bernadette's he wasn't at either place, and the telephone at the bungalow remained unanswered.

Katie came in at half-past four, full of her first day back at school, and as Leah observed her fondly there was no doubt in her mind that in this instance they had done the right thing. She was so obviously delighted to be back that her own heart filled with pleasure every time she looked at her.

'Any news on Bobby?' she whispered when they were alone in the office.

Leah shook her head.

'No, not yet, and I can't get hold of Nathan, but I'm sure he'll be in touch soon.'

'When do you think I could go to see him?' Katie asked.

'Not yet, I think. His mother is in a very anxious state, as any mother would be, and I don't think she'll want strangers around at the moment.'

'We're not strangers to Bobby and Mr Bonner,' she protested.

'No, indeed,' Leah replied, admitting to herself uneasily that it was as if she had known him all her life, instead of for just a short time, 'but we're talking about a woman who loves her son, and while in a strange country has found that he is suffering from a serious illness that may cause permanent disablement.'

Katie was frowning.

'Yes, I know that, but don't you think she's lucky to have a husband who can make him better?'

'Yes, I do,' Leah agreed gently, 'but it's what Nathan is going to have to do in the process that is distressing her so much.'

'She sounds ungrateful to me,' her sister persisted.

Leah wasn't to be drawn.

'I don't know the lady so I can't pass an opinion, but it sounds to me like the mother hen protecting her chick, and if she's getting her priorities a bit confused, who can blame her?'

Nathan for one, she thought. Maxine was giving him a rough time, and though Leah could understand her anguish, she was appalled at the burden that the

American woman was placing on him after years of
little or no contact. Had she for one moment considered what it was doing to him? It would have been
better to have let the London doctors deal with it, and
kept Nathan out of it, but he wouldn't have wanted
that, would he. . .his skills bypassed while another surgeon operated on his son? The man was in a cleft stick
and her heart ached for him, more so because he didn't
expect sympathy, because he was taking the whole
tragic affair in his stride with a dogged calm that had
her full admiration.

After they had eaten she and Katie watched television for a while, but when the younger girl started
yawning Leah suggested an early night after the
stresses and excitement of her first day back at school.
When Leah looked in on her a short time later she
was asleep, her slight frame hardly lifting the duvet,
and the piquant young face was tranquil and free
from care.

As Leah looked down on her, tenderness filled her,
and her inside knotted as she tried to visualise how
she would feel if Katie were in Bobby's position. It
didn't bear thinking about, and she went to the window
as she had already done several times during the
evening, hoping to see the car on the drive and the
bungalow ablaze with light, but it was the same as
before. . .no Nathan.

She picked up a book and started to read but the
words were meaningless, and so she decided to take
a bath and have an early night herself. Why hadn't
Nathan been in touch? she wondered as she lay in the
soft scented water. Had he had second thoughts about
divulging his private affairs to a stranger?

As she slipped quietly between her own sheets she
knew dismally that sleep was a thousand miles away.
The bath had relaxed her body, but not her mind, and
as she watched the minutes crawl by on the bedside

clock she knew it was going to be a long night.

At half-past one she padded silently into the kitchen to make a coffee, and as she was reaching out for the light switch she heard Nathan's car on the drive below. As its sleek elegance swished to a halt, her heart started to race. He was back from wherever he had been, she thought thankfully, and maybe now they could talk, though he was hardly likely to come knocking on her door at this hour with the flat in darkness. Unable to face the rest of the night without having spoken to him, she flicked down the light switch and went to the kitchen window.

He had seen the light go on and was standing at his front door looking up to where her slender figure in a long cream silk nightgown was outlined against the window.

Nathan raised his hand and she waved back, and he came striding across to the path beneath the window.

'Can I come up?' he mouthed.

'Yes,' she whispered back. 'Please do.'

She watched him walk towards the side door that led to the staircase that wound up to the flat, and this time she wasn't bothered what the night staff might think if they saw him. She was anxious to see for herself what state he was in, and even more anxious to hear what he had to say, and nothing else mattered.

By the time she had flung a robe over her nightdress he was tapping gently on the door, and as she opened it Leah felt weak and breathless. It could have been from tension, apprehension, or a myriad of other reasons, or it might just be that she hadn't seen him for two days, and that was two days too long, she thought, as her eyes devoured his face.

It was a mask of cold anger, and confusion made her glance waver. She had been prepared for pain, sorrow, grim acceptance, all of those things, but not anger. Nathan was a surgeon, he knew the score, just as would anyone else in his profession, so what was responsible for the tight jawline and the whiteness around his mouth? She was about to find out.

'Katie asleep?' he asked in a low voice as he followed her into the lounge.

'Yes, blotto,' she said with a smile.

He sank down wearily on to the sofa and she said quickly.

'I was just about to make coffee. . .?'

He leaned back and closed his eyes.

'I'd love one, Leah. My throat's parched and my stomach's empty.'

She eyed him anxiously. 'I'll make you a meal?'

He lifted his hand in protest.

'No, just the drink will be fine. I'm too churned up to eat. When I saw your light go on a few moments ago, it was like an oasis in the dark night. I never expected you to be up at this hour.'

Colour washed up in her face, but she eyed him steadily.

'I couldn't sleep because I hadn't heard from you.' And if that wasn't telling him how much he had taken over her life, she didn't know what would.

If the thought *had* occurred to him he didn't show it, he merely nodded as if that was what he would have expected, and then said bleakly, 'I'm going to have to amputate, Leah. The tests I've requested show that there *are* lesions in the lungs, to a minute degree admittedly, but it means that amputation followed by chemotherapy is the only safe option. Even that's not a hundred per cent sure, but there's every chance that it *will* save Bobby's life, and if I can do that, I'll know I haven't failed him.'

Leah wanted to go to him and put her arms around him, not as a lover, but as someone comforting a ravaged parent, and yet something held her back. Nathan must have been to hell and back during the last twenty-four hours, and maybe that was the reason for the rage she sensed in him, but she didn't think so.

'You must feel as if you're in the middle of a nightmare,' she probed cautiously.

'I didn't,' he said grimly. 'At first I was prepared to accept it as one of the hard knocks that life is always handing out to those who least deserve them, and I was just grateful to be able to do something practical to help my son. God knows I've done little enough for him.'

'That can't have all been your fault,' she reminded him gently, but he went on as if she hadn't spoken.

'Every ounce of skill I possess is at his disposal, and I thought that would be enough, but it isn't. Maxine won't give her consent for the operation to take place.'

Leah stared at him in shock. She could feel her blood chilling. Nathan was under enough pressure without that. His ex-wife must be out of her mind, completely crazy, and yet, even as she thought it, her heart went out to the anguished mother. She was clutching at straws, praying for an easier solution, and he hadn't been able to offer her one.

She went across to him and took his hand in hers, the hand that would hold the scalpel.

'That's awful, Nathan,' she breathed. 'What are you going to do?'

'Take her to court,' he said flatly, and as Leah's eyes widened, he went on, 'I have no choice. In a situation like this, the surgeon will ask that Social Services be made legal guardians, overruling the parent or parents, and allowing the surgery to go ahead. Obviously I as a parent can't give my consent, as I'm also the doctor, and so it's for Maxine to give *her* permission, which she refuses to do.' His eyes were golden flints in the pallor of his face.

'Osteosarcoma spreads very quickly. It's already got its nasty little feelers into Bobby's lungs, so there's no time to waste. Maxine and I have spent the whole day arguing. It's a good job the poor kid wasn't there to hear us. I went round to their hotel to tell her and Dex what I've decided and she hit the roof.'

'But a court hearing can take time to arrange,' she said anxiously, 'and time is something Bobby hasn't got.'

His smile was a grimace.

'*You* can see that, my darling Leah, *I* can see that, but my awkward predatory *wife* can't.'

'A lot of people behave irrationally under stress,' she reminded him, her heart aching for him, 'but I'm sure when she's had time to calm down Maxine will accept your decision. Why bring Bobby to you if she hasn't got faith in your judgement? Her opinion of you *has* to be higher than you think.'

'I doubt it,' he said drily, 'but I'm going to give her twenty-four hours, and then I shall appeal to the court, and in a case such as this they'll arrange a special hearing.'

She nodded gravely and he smiled for the first time.

'I pride myself on being the world's most self-reliant person,' he said, 'and here I am pouring out my troubles to you again. You must be weary of the sight of me.'

'No, never,' she said softly, and as his eyes warmed she ignored the clang of warning bells in her mind and told him, 'I'm only too happy to be here for you, Nathan. No one should have to carry the sort of burden you're carrying alone.'

'And who was there for *you* when you lost your home. . .and your lover?' he asked, with the tightness back in his face.

His eyes went over the dark tousled mop of her hair and the concerned blue eyes beneath it, and then they dropped to the swell of her pointed young breasts inside the silken nightwear, and he gritted savagely,

'How could you give yourself to a worthless clod like that, Leah?'

It was a question she had asked herself repeatedly in the weeks after discovering Terry's true worth, and always she had condemned herself as a fool, but she wasn't prepared to be castigated for it by someone else. As outrage rose in her, she snapped, 'It was no different from *you* marrying a selfish bossy American! Terry might have been a rotter, but he was fond of children and would never have denied a child one of its parents!'

He laughed, a low, amused sound deep in his throat, and she eyed him stonily. Only seconds ago he had been censuring her, and now it was time for poking fun, it seemed. But it wasn't quite like that. Nathan was on his feet and reaching for her, his hands warm and hard on her arms through the sleeves of the filmy negligé.

'I'm sorry,' he said, his breath fanning her cheek. 'For a moment I was foolishly consumed with pique, but, as you were so quick to point out, *my* big romance was nothing to brag about either, which I suppose makes us even, don't you think?'

He was so close, so desirable, that thinking in any shape or form was beyond her. Her senses had taken over and there was no sanity in her, no logic or reasoning. The chemistry between the sexes was rising in them and all else taking second place. Passion was blotting out his anger and weariness, his mouth was claiming hers, and as he pressed her near-nakedness against the hard strength of him Leah knew that what she had felt for Terry had been nothing compared to this. . .this exquisite rapport of feeling and escalation of pleasure.

It was then that she remembered Katie sleeping in the next room. . .and the promises she had made to herself. She had vowed that it was going to be just the two of them, no encumbrances of a romantic nature, and she drew back from his embrace.

He frowned. 'What's wrong?' and before she could reply, 'Don't tell me. Let me guess. We're violating the "touch me not" treaty?'

He was mocking her and it hurt.

'You're right as usual,' she said raggedly. 'Don't complicate my life, Nathan. I'd rather we were just friends.'

His smile was devilish.

'You mean we should swap library books and discuss our favourite TV programmes, or visit the museum together? Maybe we could go the whole hog and exchange recipes?'

She supposed she had asked for it, but it didn't make the mockery any less painful.

'Yes, and offer comfort when in distress,' she replied with quiet dignity, 'because if there is anything at all I can do to help with the problem of Bobby's illness, you have only to ask.'

He gave her a long hard look.

'You're right, of course. For a few moments, I was shelving what lies ahead. If it's friendship you want, then friendship it is, and some time when it's not so late you can explain your definition of comfort.' And the wicked smile was back.

'Go back to bed, Leah,' he ordered abruptly, and, without touching her again, he went.

She stood in the shadows and watched him stride quickly up the path, and as the door of the bungalow closed behind him, she gave a gasp of dismay. She hadn't told him about Helen Yorke! One of the residents of Barleyfields had passed away and her employer hadn't been told! Her hand went out to pick up the phone, but she hesitated. He had had enough for one night. It might as well wait until morning.

She slept eventually, but her sleep was full of dreams where Nathan pursued her relentlessly with a huge

cook-book in one hand, the thigh bone of a whale in
the other, and a copy of the *TV Times* gripped between
his teeth, doggy fashion. When he caught up with her
at last he thrust them all into her arms, but she shrank
back, refusing to take them, and in the dream he gave
a low laugh as he had done earlier, and said, 'Just
friends, eh, Leah?' and walked away.

She awoke to find Katie's slim hand on her wrist
and her worried face looking down on her.

'You were having a bad dream, Leah,' she said. 'Are
you all right?'

She struggled up on to the pillows.

'Yes, of course,' she mumbled. 'What was I saying?'

'You kept shouting, "*And* lovers. . .and lovers!"
over and over again.'

Leah managed a smile. 'Well, I'm sure I don't know
what all that was about, but I'm sorry I disturbed you.
Let's get back to sleep, shall we?'

She surfaced the next morning to a discordant duet
from the alarm clock and the telephone, and after
switching off one and picking up the other, Nathan's
voice hissed angrily in her ear.

'Leah?'

She pulled herself upright.

'Yes?'

'What the hell is going on?'

'I'm not with you,' she said, blinking drowsily.

'I've just been into the home and the night staff
informed me that Helen Yorke died yesterday.'

Leah felt herself go hot.

'Er. . .yes. . .she did.'

'Why wasn't I informed?'

'I couldn't get hold of you. I tried everywhere I
could think of.'

'Yes, well, as I told you, I was with Maxine all day,
but even so, you saw me last night.'

'Yes, I know, and I remembered the moment you'd left,' she said uncomfortably, 'but by then I felt that it was too late to bother you.'

'It is never too late to bother me with things that concern Barleyfields,' he said in the same chilly tones. 'I thought I'd made it clear that I have no intention of neglecting any of my commitments.'

'Yes, you did.'

'So, why then?'

Leah gave a silent groan. She had been dismayed enough last night when she realised that she hadn't told him about Helen, but this was awful. All right, she *was* at fault. It would be highly embarrassing for him if a member of the public should question him about Helen Yorke, and discover that the man who owned the home that she was in wasn't even aware that she had died. He had every right to be angry that he had not been informed. Now he was badgering her for a reason for her lapse, and she thought that he shouldn't need to ask. Last night he had told her that Bobby must lose his leg, and that his ex-wife wouldn't consent to the surgery, and everything else had been wiped out of her mind with the sadness of it. On top of that, she had almost ended up in his arms again. The combination of the two were reason enough, and anger started to rise in her at his inability to see that.

'I'm sorry,' she said stiffly. 'I allowed my mind to become bogged down with *your* problems instead of keeping it on my job, although you have been adamant that I shouldn't work overtime. At one o'clock in the morning I would expect to be off the hook.'

She was being unreasonable and she knew it, trying to justify herself when she was to blame, and yet it did not stop her from saying, 'In future, I will see that you are informed of everything that happens in Barleyfields.'

He gave a short amazed laugh.

'Now you're being ridiculous. I don't want to be told about everything, just matters such as this.'

'It would have been my first priority this morning, and I can assure you that kind of oversight won't happen again. Now, if you'll excuse me, I must get up and prepare for work, otherwise there will be another black mark against me for unpunctuality.'

There was silence for a moment, and then he said in the tone one would use to a fractious child, 'Now you really *are* being ridiculous.'

He was right, she was, and it wasn't clear in her mind whether it was because she was peeved at herself for giving him cause for complaint, or because she felt humiliated at Nathan seeing her as anything less than efficient. His good opinion mattered. . .it mattered a lot.

'Maybe I am,' she agreed tonelessly. 'I've been ridiculous on a few occasions recently——' and most of them have been when *you've* touched me, she thought grimly '—but it won't happen again.'

'It's quite obvious that you've got out of the wrong side of the bed,' he said drily.

'That's where you're wrong,' she flung back at him. 'I'm still in it, and shouldn't be at this hour, so I'll say goodbye.'

CHAPTER SEVEN

As THE day progressed with its busy routine, the routine that Leah had adjusted to so well, she was grateful to have her mind occupied. The early morning exchange of words with Nathan had left her feeling dispirited and on edge, as it had made her realise fully just how much she had let him into her life. As she had prepared a hasty breakfast for Katie and herself, she had seen clearly that the only way to banish the turmoil in her mind was to keep out of Nathan's affairs.

It was the afternoon when the hairdresser came, an event of some importance, when an assortment of heads in varying shades of grey were washed and trimmed, and in the case of the ladies either permed or set. Mabel had decided to have a perm, which according to Suzie was unheard of, as she usually kept her thick white locks in a neat straight cut.

When she sallied forth from one of the bedrooms that had been turned into a salon for the afternoon, Giles gave a low whistle of approval and the rose in her cheeks deepened.

'That's enough, you cheeky young rip,' she said with her usual chuckle.

Leah, who had been standing nearby observing the transformation, said warmly, 'You look lovely, Mabel.'

'Do you think this has something to do with Thomas Whateley, Sister?' Giles asked innocently. 'I've noticed that he's in the front lounge more than he's in his own suite.'

'Get away with you,' the old woman said with a tolerant laugh as she made her slow way back to her seat and her crocheting.

Jean and Jack had also enjoyed the ministrations of the hairdresser, and as they came out, together as always, Leah's experienced eye saw the plump little woman stagger. She was beside her in an instant.

'What is it, Jean?' she asked, guiding her to the nearest chair, with her husband still clutching her hand.

'I don't know, Sister,' she said slowly, slurring her words. 'I went all dizzy for a moment.'

Jack was watching her, panic in his eyes, and Leah said unhurriedly, 'Yes, well, I think perhaps you need to lie down for a little while. You'll feel better after you've rested,' and to Annette Pryce who had just arrived on the scene, 'Will you and one of the others get Jean to bed, please, Annette?' As the difficult RGN nodded without speaking, Leah went to phone for a doctor.

The diagnosis was a slight stroke in layman's terms, in the doctor's words a transient ischaemic attack, a warning that sufficient blood supply wasn't getting to the brain.

'Give her aspirin twice daily,' he said, 'and the lady needs to diet, she's overweight. . .not active enough. At the moment there seems to no loss of use in the limbs, or signs of dysarthria or hemianopia, that is, impairment of speech, or the loss of half the field of vision, which are all good signs. I'll call in again tomorrow.' As he had surveyed the hovering husband, he had said quietly, 'If me laddo doesn't calm down, he'll be the next.'

Leah nodded.

'A sedative?' she suggested.

'Why not? At least he'll get a good night's sleep, and if he's still overwrought in the morning, I'd keep him mildly sedated for a few days.'

In the late afternoon Leah was in the office working on the staff rota for the coming week, and when she looked up Nathan was standing in the doorway holding a florist's bouquet of deep red roses. He was eyeing her consideringly over the scarlet perfection of the flowers. When he offered them to her she was filled with gladness, and the day's niggling doubts and irritations disappeared. Nathan had brought her flowers. . .her instincts had been right. . .she *hadn't* read too much into their relationship, and as she looked at him with shining eyes, Annette came sidling past to get to the drugs cupboard.

As she took the flowers from him, her mouth soft and tender at his thoughtful gesture, Leah was conscious of the other woman's green eyes boring into her back, and she wished her a thousand miles away. Even more so when he said uninterestedly, 'The man from the florists and I almost collided on the step and I said I'd see that you got them.'

Nathan raised a sardonic eyebrow and Annette sniggered behind her as Leah stammered in scalding embarrassment, 'So they're *not* from. . .?' 'You' she'd been going to say, but had bitten the word back just in time.

'There's a card with them,' he said, as if stating the obvious was a necessary boring chore.

'Yes, of course,' she replied quickly, trying to gather her wits as her eyes focused on a small cardboard square clearly visible through the cellophane. It said, 'Can you forgive me, Leah, darling?' and underneath a name. . .'Terry.'

Terry! The name sprang out at her as if in lights and, speechless with anger and dismay, she read it again, knowing that Nathan could see the words just as clearly as she. There hadn't been a sign of Terry since the day she had handed over the money from the sale of the cottage, and now he was rearing his objectionable head again, just when she'd discovered what it was like to care for a real man. . .the one that she thought had brought her the flowers.

She placed the bouquet carefully on the desk, handling it as if it might be poison ivy instead of red roses, and said stiffly, 'If you'll excuse me, I have work to do,' and added, her face expressionless, 'and as regards that, *and* as promised, I'm informing you that Jean Garside has had a slight stroke.' She walked out of the office with a determined attempt at dignity, aware that even before she had left the room Annette was smiling up at Nathan and he was bending attentively towards the woman who already had him labelled as her second 'Mr Right'.

When Katie came hurtling into the flat at teatime, having stayed behind for netball practice, her first words threw Leah into further confusion.

'I've just seen Mr Bonner on the drive,' she said, 'and I asked him when we could visit Bobby.'

'You did?' Leah said slowly.

'Yes, and he said tonight would be a good time, as once he's had the operation it might not be so convenient. So shall we go, Leah?'

'I don't know,' she said, wilting at the thought of any further confrontations with Nathan.

Katie was staring at her in surprise.

'Surely you want to see Bobby?' she questioned.

'Of course I do,' Leah told her tartly. 'It's just that. . .'

'Just what? I thought you liked Bobby and his dad.'

'I do, and of course we'll go, just as soon as we've eaten.'

She was just as anxious to see the boy as Katie was, so why let the idiosyncrasies of the fathers wash off on to the children?

They found Bobby in bed watching television, and Leah was relieved to see that he was alone.

'Katie! Sure is good to see ya,' he exclaimed, and

Leah had to smile at her own sudden invisibility.

'And Leah,' he said as a respectful afterthought, and
they all began to laugh.

She had been dreading that the imperious Maxine
might be there, even though she was overwhelmingly
curious about Nathan's ex-wife, but she reminded herself that keeping out of his affairs was today's decision.
What tomorrow's would be remained to be seen. If
visiting Nathan's son was keeping out of his affairs she
would eat her hat, she thought wryly.

When she commented tactfully on the fact that he
was alone, Bobby switched his attention from Katie
for a second to explain that Mom and Pops had just
gone and wouldn't be back until later.

'And. . . Dad?'

'He's been around most of the day, but he got a
bleep not long ago and had to go.'

So Nathan had returned to St Bernadette's after the
fiasco in the office, and then some sort of emergency
had caused him to leave. Maybe it was Annette need-
ing resuscitation, she thought unreasonably, as they
had both forgotten her the moment she had started to
leave the office.

As she sat quietly watching the two teenagers
chattering away, Leah wondered if Bobby was aware
of the trauma going on behind the scenes with regard
to himself. She doubted it, but thought that even if he
was, he would probably take it in the same manner as
he had accepted everything else. Whatever faults his
mother might have, she had brought him up to be an
extremely pleasant and well adjusted boy, and not
every parent could boast of that.

As they were preparing to leave, with Katie having
promised to come again soon, the door opened and
Leah saw that the curiosity that she had been prepared
to shelve was about to be satisfied.

A man and woman were coming into the room and

it did not need two guesses as to who they were. The
big shape of the man was a blur. Leah's eyes were
riveted on the woman, and all her preconceived ideas
about Nathan's ex-wife went by the board.

The most striking features of her were her hair which
hung heavy and corn-coloured on to her shoulders,
and the cool grey eyes. She was expensively dressed,
a cross between Harrods and Neiman Marcus, Leah
thought, but apart from that she was quite plain.

She stood there, waiting for them to make themselves known, but not so the man at her side. He was
tanned and smiling, and he held out a big paw and
said in a soft drawl, 'I'm Dexter Schultz, and this is
my wife, Maxine, and you'll be. . .?'

Leah cleared her throat. This was an ill-timed meeting, but it had occurred, and it was up to her to make
the best of it.

'I'm Leah Morgan,' she said pleasantly, 'and this is
my young sister, Katie.'

'Dad and I went to see *Jurassic Park* with Leah and
Katie,' Bobby chipped in.

'Ah! So you're the little nurse Nathan talks about,'
Maxine Schultz drawled. 'Seems as if you're on his
side. You think I should heed him?'

'We *all* do, darlin',' the big man said. 'You know
Nathan can't take chances with the boy.'

Leah cast a quick glance at Bobby, but he and Katie
were chatting again and he was taking scant notice,
but she nevertheless felt that this was not the place
for the kind of discussion that his mother had started.

She swallowed uncomfortably. This meeting was
going to be even more awkward than she had antici-
pated, and she had a strong desire to be gone, but the
woman's grey eyes were fixed on her and there was
something in their gaze that demanded an answer.

'I think that Nathan is right in what he is proposing
to do, Mrs Schultz,' she said quietly, 'but don't you

think we ought to discuss it outside?'

'Sure,' she agreed, and the three of them went out
into the corridor, where Maxine said immediately with
the same cold control that she had been displaying in
the sick room, 'You're a nurse, so maybe you know
somethin' we don't, eh?'

'I'm afraid not,' Leah assured her. 'Not medically,
anyway, but you will already have been told by various
doctors, including Nathan, how life-threatening
Bobby's illness is?'

She saw the American woman flinch, and underneath her make-up she was deathly pale. She nodded
mutely, and suddenly Leah's apprehension vanished.
In a strange sort of way, she felt in control.

'Mrs Schultz. . .' she began.

'My name's Maxine,' she said stonily.

'All right. . . Maxine. Have you thought that Nathan
is going to have to remember for the rest of his life
that he had to amputate Bobby's leg? It will be a
horrendous burden, but he's strong and resilient, and
I know he will cope, mainly because he'll know that,
although he couldn't save his leg, he did everything
possible to save his life.'

Maxine nodded again, reluctantly, and the grey eyes
flickered as Leah went on, 'But with regard to yourself
and your refusal to give consent for the operation, the
burden on *your* shoulders will make his seem light if
Bobby should lose his life because you wouldn't let
Nathan operate. Your son's life would be gone, your
own ruined, as well as that of your husband if he had
to stand by and witness your never-ending guilt. I don't
doubt he could cope with your grief, but guilt is a
different ballgame, Maxine.'

Leah could scarcely believe that the words were
coming from *her* own mouth. She was lecturing the
distraught mother in no uncertain terms, and they had
only met a few moments ago. She knew why, of course.

She loved Nathan Bonner. It was as simple as that.

There was a heavy silence in the corridor when she had finished speaking, and then Maxine said grimly, 'I guess you're right. I don't have a choice, do I?'

'No, you don't, Maxie,' Dexter said. 'Neither does young Bobby. . .or Nathan.'

Her eyes were on Leah.

'You can tell Nathan to fetch me the papers.'

'Tell him yourself,' she said gently. 'That's what he would want. I've just been a friend with a listening ear, that's all. There's no need for him to know that *I've* been involved in your decision, Maxine.' She took the older woman's slim, manicured hand in hers. 'I feel for you all so much, and wish there was something I could do to help.'

'You *have* helped, more than you'll ever know,' the big Texan said, with an anxious glance at his wife, and as Leah called Katie to her, the couple went back into Bobby's room.

On the way home, Leah was silent and Katie asked, 'What was all that about in the corridor, Leah?'

'Just a chat about Bobby's illness, that's all,' she said, conjuring up a smile.

She didn't feel like smiling. She felt low and depressed. For one thing she had got herself involved in Nathan's affairs again, on the face of it to good effect, but who would want a pat on the back for persuading a grieving mother to agree to the amputation of her child's leg?

Hopefully she had done something to lessen Nathan's misery, but it had increased someone else's. Yet was that not how it always was with this kind of situation? The operation could go ahead now with all speed, and once it was over, all of them, including herself, could get on with their lives. The Schultz family would go back to London. She and Katie would settle into a peaceful routine. . .and Nathan? Well, for one thing, he would have more contact with his son, at least while the family were in England, and that could only be good. For the rest of it, he would no doubt get back into routine, and if her cowardly insistence that there should be only friendship between them became part of that routine, she wouldn't complain.

She had admitted to herself back there at the hospital that she loved him. There were no doubts in her mind about that, but there was nothing to show that he felt the same, and with regards to herself, she needed time, things between them had been moving too fast, and after Terry. . .!

Her thoughts went back to his ill-timed peace offering. He had a nerve! It would have been bad enough to receive the flowers from him if she had been alone, but to have to accept them in front of Nathan and the tittering Annette was the final straw.

Whatever the message had been on Nathan's bleeper while at St Bernadette's, he was at Barleyfields when they got back, chatting to Anne Mirfield in the front porch, his face and the dark bronze of his hair clearly visible beneath the light.

'There's Mr Bonner,' Katie said, as they drove past.

'Yes, so I see.'

'Bobby's lucky to have two such super fathers, isn't he?' her sister said wistfully.

'Mm,' Leah agreed, 'but yours is all right, isn't he?'

Katie laughed.

'Yes, *he's* super, too, but I just wish he hadn't put someone in Mum's place so soon.'

'I don't think it means he loved her any less, you know,' Leah said. 'It's just the way he is. Dad can't stand loneliness.'

'He had us.'

Yes, but we didn't warm his bed, Leah thought.

Katie had gone upstairs, and she was locking the car when Nathan's voice came from behind.

'Where've you been, Leah?' he asked.

'To see Bobby,' she told him briefly.

'Not to bestow forgiveness on an old boyfriend, then?'

'*No. . .I . . . have. . .not!*' she said stiffly. 'And even if I had, what's it got to do with you?'

He regarded her steadily.

'Not a lot. I just don't want to see you make a fool of yourself again.'

'Gee, thanks!' she snapped.

With his talent for raising her hackles and then changing the subject, he asked calmly, 'Did you see Maxine and Dex?'

'Only briefly. They were arriving as we were leaving.'

It was the truth, a reduced version of it, but still the truth.

'And?'

'And what? When we introduced ourselves, she asked if I was the little nurse you'd mentioned.'

He grinned.

'I felt like a wet-behind-the-ears probationer.'

'Never that. . . Sister! Never that! You're more than a match for anyone.'

'Including yourself?'

That dangerous light was in his eyes again. 'But of course. I'm putty in your hands.'

It was her turn to be amused. 'Oh, yes? Well, you must be short on linseed oil, as you don't seem very malleable to me.'

A car hooted behind them and in the gloom Leah was just able to make out Dexter Schultz behind the wheel. This was the moment to make herself scarce, she thought, and as Maxine gave her a wintry smile through the car window Leah put her finger to her lips in a gesture of silence, and then, as Nathan walked over to them, she flew up the stairs.

He came knocking on the door an hour later, and as soon as she saw his face, Leah knew that he was aware of Maxine's decision. She only hoped that her own name hadn't come into the conversation. It seemed not.

'Maxine has had a change of mind, Leah,' he said thankfully, as they stood in the small hallway. 'God! What a relief! I won't have to start proceedings now.' He ran his hand through the thick crop of his hair. 'I've just phoned and booked the theatre for three o'clock tomorrow. That was the first empty slot.'

'That's good news, Nathan,' she said sombrely. 'I'm glad that she's reconciled to what must happen. She's lucky to have that nice husband of hers beside her at a time like this.'

'Yes, isn't she?' he said, and they were both aware that the same didn't apply to him. *He* was alone.

She could feel her arms wanting to go out to him, but she drew back. The moment they touched it would be there, the electricity, the current that set her on fire.

His eyes darkened and the strong mouth curved into a grim smile. 'It's OK, Leah, darling. I *can* cope. I'm going to have it engraved on my tombstone. . ."HE COPED".'

His hand brushed her cheek for a second and then he went.

Katie was in the kitchen making cocoa.

'Who was that?' she wanted to know.

'Nathan,' she told her briefly.

'Oh, I see,' and then, 'Do you think Bobby will be as dishy as his dad when he grows up?'

Leah smiled.

'I'm sure I don't know, although he's very much like him already.'

'Nathan Bonner seems to be around a lot,' Katie remarked. 'Are you and he. . .?'

'What?'

'You know. . .in love?'

'Of course, not.'

'Well, you could have kidded me,' she said with a grin. 'He smoulders every time he looks at you.'

Leah felt her colour rise.

'You've been reading too many novelettes, my girl,' she told her.

As the clock hung before three the following afternoon Leah told Giles, who was icing a birthday cake for one of the elderlies, and the only person around at the time, 'If anyone needs me, I'm going into the garden for a little while.'

Engrossed in the task, he nodded, and she slipped out through the side door. It was a warmer afternoon than those past and she made her way to a seat beside a grassy slope dotted with daffodils.

A church clock in the distance struck three, and she thought that Bobby and Nathan would be in Theatre now, and that was why she had come outside. She didn't want to bring her mind to bear on the problems of the young while surrounded by the old.

He was of no age to have to face what was about to happen to him, and she prayed that he would soon be over it and able to get on with his life. . .a healthy one.

Leah had brought herself up to date with what the surgery would entail. For one thing, she was curious from a medical point of view, but another far more important reason was that, if Nathan should want to talk about it in detail, there would be no comfort for him in discussing it with someone only half informed.

Obviously she had dealt with amputees at St Bridget's in Women's Surgical, and had seen how a neat flap of skin and muscle was left below the cut, to be sewn into a compact protective cover for the stump. In a nursing capacity, she had supervised th healing process, where bandaging and plaster casts were used to mould the end of the limb into a suitable shape for the prosthesis to be attached, an event which usually came about six weeks after the surgery. In many cases, artificial limbs were now kept in place by suction instead of straps which, for a young boy such as Bobby, would be far less harassing to deal with.

Nathan would have checked for the presence of any abnormal arrangement of blood vessels caused by the tumour, with angiography, and also found out what the skin temperature was through thermography, before operating. Once that had been done, the blood vessels would be tied off and the bone sawn through.

She could visualise him in his theatre greens, the tawny eyes missing nothing, his hand rock-steady. . . and his heart aching, only *she* knew how much. She longed to be there for him when it was over, but how would Maxine feel about Nathan's 'little nurse' appearing on the scene at a time of great stress in their lives? Not too chuffed, she'd like to bet, and who could blame her. Yet *she* had the comforting Dex to turn to, while Nathan. . .

'Sister!' Giles was at the door, spatula in hand, a blob of icing sugar on his nose. 'There's a relative on the phone wants a word with you.'

'Right, I'm coming.' she called back, and Barleyfields took over once more.

Katie was staying the night at a schoolfriend's that night and so Leah ate alone. Even before she had finished her meal, she knew that she was going to the hospital. The way she felt had nothing to do with sexual chemistry. It stemmed from a deep compassionate love, a love that was new. . .and unwelcome. She hadn't planned to lose her heart again, not so so soon, anyway, but she had reckoned without meeting a man like Nathan Bonner. If there was even the remotest chance that he might need her, she must be there.

The reception area of the private patients' wing was deserted except for a smartly dressed girl on the desk. When Leah stated her business, she gave a pleasant smile and pointed the way towards the room where she and Katie had visited Bobby the previous evening.

As Leah padded quietly along the carpeted corridor a figure dressed in the green garb of the operating theatre came out of a side passage in front of her, and without turning his head in her direction moved swiftly towards Bobby's room. The shape and stance of him were unmistakable.

'Nathan!' she called, her voice squeaky with nerves and tension.

He didn't hear her. His hand was already on the doorknob, and as she hurried to catch up with him he flung it open and she heard him say heavily, 'It's done, Maxine. I've done what I had to do. You can go to him. He's in the recovery ward.' As Leah came up behind him in the doorway, he held out his arms to the woman standing tensely by the window and she went into them like a homing bird.

Neither of them were aware of her presence, she could have been a million miles away. As Leah turned to go, she glimpsed Dexter slumped in an armchair, watching them with a wry smile.

As she went through the swing doors and out into the chill night, Leah wondered if he had been thinking the same as she: that their presence was surplus to requirements.

Walking back to the flat, she saw a cinema queue and joined it listlessly. It would be somewhere to spend a couple of hours instead of being alone, and when she came out, remembering little of the film, a coffee-bar nearby provided a place to idle away another hour.

Stirring a lukewarm coffee, Leah had to admit that her dejection was outweighed by the relief of knowing that Bobby's operation was over. Tonight she had felt very much on the fringe of Nathan's life, which was exactly where she was, but, although an outsider, she would still have been deeply concerned for the boy even if she *hadn't* been in love with his father. That the parents should gravitate towards each other at such a time was only to be expected, she thought wistfully, and wished she could stop thinking about that fine dividing line between hate and love.

'I can cope,' Nathan had said in his concise manner, and she had known it to be true, yet she had still wanted to think he might need her. Terry's weakly handsome face came into her mind and she knew that *he* would need her. She would have to be the strong one for *him*, and bringing him to mind took her back to the moment when Nathan had placed his untimely and unwelcome bouquet in her arms. The last thing she wanted was Terry trying to wheedle his way back into her life. *He* was yesterday's bad news, and the man who owned Barleyfields was today's *good* news.

The only problem was that it could be all on her side, that she was letting her heart take over from her head, and as exhaustion washed over her, Leah left the coffee-bar. With Nathan's admonitions about being alone on the streets at night in mind, she hailed a passing taxi.

It was almost midnight when she got back. The bungalow was deserted as she had thought it might be. Nathan was hardly likely to come galloping back home the second he had operated on his son. It was to be expected that he and the Schultzes would stay the night, to be there for the boy during the first few hours after he had regained consciousness, and also, as far as Nathan was concerned, to be on hand in his role of surgeon should he be needed.

As she lay upon her soft single divan, Leah wished that Katie was home. She felt lonely and unloved, and at the same time ashamed at giving in to self-pity.

CHAPTER EIGHT

GILES rang in sick the next morning and Leah designated Suzie and Annette to kitchen duty. They accepted the temporary arrangement gracefully enough, and Leah filled in to make up for their absence from their usual duties.

When she had gone into the office on arriving, Leah had found the bouquet from Terry on the desk where she had left it, the roses looking worse for wear from lack of water. She had picked it up and taken it outside to the dustbin. As she had slammed the lid down on it, she had wished it were Terry that she was delegating to the rubbish heap instead of his flowers.

In the middle of the afternoon the birthday cake that Giles had been working on the previous day was to be presented to a sprightly though somewhat vacant eighty-year-old, and all the staff had gathered in the front lounge to sing 'Happy Birthday'.

Leah was on the point of joining them when the doorbell rang, and she hurried along the deserted hallway to answer it. Terry was standing in the porch, eyeing her with the dark, appealing eyes that had hidden a deceitful and calculating mind.

She reeled back.

'Did you get the flowers?' he asked, with his little-boy smile.

Her face was deathly white. How dared he come to Barleyfields? 'Yes, I did,' she hissed, pulling the door to behind her. 'How did you know where I was?'

'I went to St Biddy's and made a few enquiries.'

'You're disgusting!' she spat. 'Just go away from

129

here. I thought I'd made it clear that I didn't want to see you again. . .ever!'

They were on the path now and it was all Leah could do to keep her hands off him.

He shrugged his shoulders.

'All right,' he agreed sulkily, 'if that's how you feel, but I've got a job now.'

'Really? And what sort of a crooked set-up is it this time?'

'It's legit, Leah,' he wheedled. 'Honestly. That other business has taught me a lesson. It scared me. I won't do it again.'

'Scared you, did it?' she raged. 'And what do you think it did to me? It made me feel dirty, and *you* introduced me to poverty. I'll never forgive you for either of those things.'

He turned to go and, beside herself with anger, she grasped his arm and pulled him back.

'I mean it, Terry. Just keep away from me in future!'

Footsteps sounded on the drive and when she looked up Nathan was coming towards them. Her heart started to hammer with dismay. Why did he have to appear at this moment? Next to Terry in his gaudy track suit, Nathan looked trim and immaculate in a light grey tweed. At any other moment, it would have gladdened her heart to see him.

There was not a vestige of a smile on his face. He looked taut and angry, and Leah wondered if it was because he had seen her drag Terry back. Even as she squirmed at the thought, the man in her grasp murmured, 'For old times' sake, eh, Leah?' and gave her a quick hard kiss on the mouth.

Before she could push him away, Nathan was stalking past them towards the open doorway with just a cold nod in her direction, but before he had barely had time to get inside, he was bellowing her name like an enraged bull.

'Leah!'

She swung round in alarm and got the smell of acrid smoke in her nostrils. The alarm changed to terror, and as she charged inside, the hallway was full of the pungent odour. When she got to the kitchen door, Nathan was beating out flames on the top of the big gas hob, and Suzie was helping a surprised-looking old lady away from the smoke and fumes.

'I was only drying the towels,' she protested mildly.

Suzie rolled her eyes above the culprit's head.

'She had only turned on all the jets of the hotplate and piled the tea-towels on top.'

Leah groaned. 'Any other day Giles would have been here,' she said dismally, 'and the other girls are at the birthday celebration. Get her outside into the fresh air,' she suggested, 'while I. . .'

'While you *what*?' Nathan asked from behind her, his voice like a whiplash. 'While you cavort on the drive with the boyfriend and let the place burn down? I was under the impression that you were in charge of Barleyfields. That the old folk were in your care.'

She was cringing as if the whip were in his hand instead of his voice.

'I consider this to be rank carelessness, Leah, and I'm not prepared to overlook it.' He lowered his voice so that the dismayed members of staff gathered nearby could not hear him. 'I suppose he's the reason for you not being around last night. So much for the clap-trap of friends being there for each other.'

She swallowed and there was a huge lump in her throat.

'You're very quick to judge me, aren't you?' she whispered back.

'No, just quick to see the obvious,' he gritted.

'I think you'd better have my notice,' she said weakly.

Surprise flashed across his face for the briefest of

moments and then he said sardonically, 'Why? Got a cardboard box lined up, have you, and one for Katie?'

'That was a fatuous remark!' she said coldly.

'Yes, but you got the point of it if your face was anything to go by. *Do* you want to be homeless and jobless, because you're going the right way about it?'

Leah turned swiftly.

'Would you mind carrying on with your duties, everyone,' she asked of the captive audience, and when the avid listeners had reluctantly departed, said, 'No, I don't, but neither do I want to be dressed down in front of those under me. I admit I'm to blame, but I was hardly likely to know that one of our ladies would get up to mischief in those few seconds.'

She had deliberately not mentioned Terry. Nathan had obviously put two and two together and made five, and if that was how he wanted it, she wasn't going to humiliate herself by explaining. Terry had been a jinx in her life before and was continuing to be so, but she had given him his marching orders and if he dared show his face again. . .!

The tawny eyes were still flashing fire.

'Maybe, but you're supposed to anticipate that kind of thing, which is easy enough when one's mind is on the job. All my staff are aware that I won't countenance men friends hanging around the place. I wouldn't have thought I needed to spell it out for *you*.'

The appeal of the cardboard box was increasing by the second, and so was her despair. Wherever had she got the idea that there could be something between them? He was arrogant, but she already knew that, his confidence and style were part of the attraction. He was intolerant. . .though not always, having seen him with Bobby and the old folks, *and* he was too quick to judge, a fault that had surfaced in recent days.

'I'm not going to start justifying myself, Nathan,'

she said frostily. '*You've* already done the judge and
jury bit. I've admitted I'm at fault and I'm sorry. As
I've already said, if you want my notice, you can
have it.'

'I'll give it my consideration,' he said with equal
coldness, and flicked a charred remnant of tea-towel
from his lapel.

'Yes, do that,' she said equably. 'In the meantime,
I'll get on with the job that I perform so badly.'

She wanted to ask him about Bobby. It was incredible that they were having this slanging match. That
there was no mention of the things that mattered, such
as how was his son. . .and Maxine. . .and what about
himself? Was the agony any less? And why was he
doing *this*. . . ripping her apart. . .wiping out the
sweet rapport they had shared?

For someone who had hardly been off her doorstep
since they'd met, Nathan managed to do an excellent
job of avoiding her after the bust-up in the office. If
he had reason to visit Barleyfields, he came in the
evening when she was off duty, and his comings and
goings from St Bernadette's were just as unlikely to
result in them meeting.

On the evening of the bonfire in the kitchen, Katie
had been keen to visit Bobby, and had tried to coax
Leah to ring his father to ask if it would be convenient
for them to go to see him.

'Ring him yourself, Katie,' Leah had told her
wearily. '*I've* had enough of that man today.'

Her sister came back from the phone disappointed.

'Mr Bonner says perhaps later in the week. Bobby's
making good progress, but he has a slight temperature
which could mean an infection.'

'Well, there you are, then,' Leah had said, hiding
her relief. She was just as anxious as Katie to see the
boy, but if their visit should end up as a package with

Maxine and Dexter and a glowering Nathan. . .she would rather give it a miss.

In the middle of Sunday morning the phone rang and Nathan's clipped voice spoke in her ear. 'Is that you, Leah?'

'Yes?'

'It's OK to visit Bobby any time you like.'

Her heart had twisted at the sound of his voice, but meeting coolness with coolness she asked, 'How is he?'

'Fine, and looking forward to seeing Katie.'

'Good,' she replied with the same sort of brevity. 'She's out at the moment, but when she gets back we'll sort something out.'

'Do that,' he said abruptly, and was gone before she had had time to ask him what he was going to do about her notice.

She had got up that morning with a sore throat, and in spite of dosing herself it was not going away. By the time Katie came back from a friend's house and they had had lunch, she was feeling hot and feverish, and knew there was no way she could go visiting the sick.

Katie was all agog at the thought of seeing Bobby, and when Leah told her that she did not feel well enough to go, her face fell.

'Can't I go on my own?' she begged.

'Yes, if you want to, as long as it's in the daylight,' Leah agreed, 'but I'm sure I'll be all right by tomorrow, if you'll wait.'

'OK,' Katie conceded, and the visit was postponed.

But on Monday morning Leah felt worse rather than better, and she went downstairs at eight o'clock to explain that she had picked up a flu bug and was going back to bed. Her plans went by the board for within five minutes, four members of staff had phoned in sick with similar symptoms to her own.

The agency could only offer one temp, and so, feeling decidedly below par, she commenced the work of the day.

The bug persisted for the rest of the week, with Katie fussing over her like a sweet small hen, and the visit to Bobby was shelved again.

On Friday morning, Leah found herself watching the clock and wondering if she was going to be able to get through the day without keeling over. The flu wasn't as bad as it had been, but she felt weak and lifeless, and envisaged a few more days before the antibiotics she had been taking took their full effect.

It would soon be the weekend, she thought thankfully, and she could stay in bed. So far Katie had escaped the virus, and Leah hoped that wearing a fine gauze mask while dealing with the old folk would have prevented any of *them* from catching it.

At five minutes before five, she was tidying up the office and filling in the report book when she heard Nathan's voice outside in the hall. Her heart started to thud. Was this the moment when he was going to tell her that he had accepted her rashly made offer of resignation, or had he come to do a quick check to see if she had committed any further misdemeanours? Whatever the reason for his presence, she knew she didn't want to see him. For one thing, she looked ghastly, and for another, if he couldn't find her, he couldn't sack her.

When she popped her head round the door he was talking to Thomas Whateley and had his back to her. Taking advantage of the fact, Leah scuttled down the passage and into the laundry room near the back door. He wouldn't think of looking for her there, that was, if he *had* come to see her, and in any case, if he did find her, it was now five o'clock, she was off duty, the weekend staff were already arriving.

'What are you doing in here?' he asked from the doorway, in a milder tone than the one he had used at their last meeting, and she wondered miserably if the future held anything other than censure on his part and misery on hers. His next words did nothing to banish the thought from her mind.

'What does it look like?' she asked tartly, and, making a gesture, she picked up the iron and plugged it in.

'It looks as if you've time for everything except a sick boy,' he said coldly. 'Promises, promises, eh, Leah? But you don't keep them, do you? If you're at odds with me, don't take it out on Bobby.'

She had felt ill all day and this just finished her off, but there was no way she was going to flake out in front of his lordship. He was a past master at putting out fires, he had extinguished the one in the kitchen, and now he had slaked out the flame he had lit in her. He could get lost.

When she lifted her head, his expression changed and she saw concern in his eyes. He started to move towards her.

'What's wrong, Leah? Are you ill?'

'No, I'm fine,' she slammed back, and dodging round the other side of the ironing board, she staggered out.

He was on her heels, hands outstretched to detain her.

'Leah, what is it?'

She struck out at his restraining hand.

'Don't touch me!' she said between clenched teeth. 'You're determined to see wrong in everything I do and that's fine by me, but in future, unless you *are* intending getting rid of me, just get off my back, will you, and let me get on with the job as well as I know how. With regards to Bobby, yes, I am ill, and I'm sure the last thing you'd want is for me to be breathing germs all over him!'

He was observing her without speaking, his intense brown gaze unsure for once, but she had not finished.

'Katie hasn't been to the hospital because I wouldn't allow her out alone in the evenings, and so our visit to Bobby hasn't materialised so far, but once I'm better it will. And do me a favour, will you, Nathan? Make sure that you're not around when we go.' On that sour note of triumph at getting in the last word, she turned her back on him and went up the stairs to the flat without a second glance.

The disdainful exit fell flat the moment she walked into her lounge. The iron! She hadn't unplugged it. If Nathan saw that, it would be the last straw. He would never accept that she was efficiency personified until *he* appeared on the scene.

There was no sign of him as she padded quietly down the stairs and flew into the laundry room to remove the plug. She breathed a sigh of relief that he had gone, but as she passed the office door she froze. He was sitting in the chair behind the desk, but she didn't need to worry, his eyes were closed and his head resting on his hands.

The following morning there was a heavy manila envelope lying on the mat and the note inside it said,

Dear Leah,

Hope that your malady is improving, along with your temper. I don't normally take orders, but in this instance am prepared to pander to your aversion to me, and will 'get off your back' while at the same time 'getting lost', although I can't promise to do the latter entirely as I own Barleyfields, live nearby, and work in the town, which is not too far away. However, it shouldn't be too difficult as, once Bobby is safely over this, I have another lecture tour planned.

If Katie and yourself care to visit Bobby in the evenings, your social life permitting, you will find

me absent. I can't guarantee the same for Maxine
and Dex, but presumably you have no quarrel
with *them*.

I've decided not to accept your notice for various
reasons, so will you please carry on as before?

Regards,
N. Bonner.

Her face crumpled. 'N. Bonner'. He couldn't get
any more formal than that! But what did she expect?
She had made it very clear the day before how she
wanted their relationship, if any, to be. It had been
the end of something sweet and magical between them,
like a flower nipped in the bud by vicious circumstance,
along with his disparagement of her.

Just be thankful that you didn't fall into another
disastrous entanglement, she told herself, but she
wasn't thankful. . .she was acutely miserable.

First, there had been Terry, plausible and dishonest,
followed by Nathan, with his devastating charm and
drive. He had been the exact opposite: honest, straight-
forward. Yes, he had been that all right! A
self-opinionated ramrod who, in his own way, had
proved just as unreliable as his predecessor, because
she never knew whether he was going to lift her up
or cast her down. She was better off without him. So
why did the bright spring morning seem dull, and the
fulfilling day ahead in Barleyfields, a chore?

Katie was eyeing her anxiously and she managed a
smile; after all, there was *one* good thing in his note.
She still had a job. They had still got a roof over their
heads, and she supposed she would have to survive
on that.

After that, the weeks developed a pattern. Nathan
went back to calling in at Barleyfields during the day
again, and, if Leah noted that it was far more

frequently than before, she put it down to his determination to let her see who was the boss, and that his finger was well and truly on the pulse.

They conversed on all matters, with the exception of themselves, with a guarded politeness, and on some occasions she found him regarding her with a perplexed uneasy stare, but when she fixed her bland blue gaze on him he immediately looked away.

She had thrown off the flu bug, but was still pale and eating very little, both factors that she knew were related to inner misery rather than the infection.

Nathan appeared to be on very good terms with Annette, something she had not been aware of previously, and the RGN was positively basking in the sunshine of his regard. So that when Gordon Bell stopped by one morning to repeat the invitation to visit him and his family, Leah found herself accepting the invitation with much more enthusiasm than she would have done, because Nathan was observing them stonily from the doorway of the office.

He made no comment, however, and she thought grimly that he had got the message. *His* only connection with her was inside Barleyfields. For the rest of it, her life was her own, which was no big deal.

She and Katie had started visiting Bobby three evenings each week and Nathan was never to be seen. Maxine and Dex were always there, which was only to be expected, and when Leah questioned the Schultzes as to whether she and Katie were in the way, Nathan's ex-wife said, 'Gee, no. Bobby needs some young company; just me and his daddy all the time is no company for the boy.'

She saw the question in Leah's eyes and picked up on it immediately. 'OK, his stepdaddy. His own daddy flits in and out, keeping a watchful eye on him, and he's not happy. I'm still devastated, but now it's done I'm acceptin' it, but Nathan. . .he looks as if he's

changed places with me. . .unless it's somethin' else
that's buggin' him.'

The cool grey eyes were observing her thoughtfully.

'Are you an' he a couple?' she drawled.

Leah's face flamed.

'No,' she said quickly, 'nothing like that,' and,
unable to keep the regret out of her voice, 'just
employer and employee.'

'Pity,' Maxine said and Leah stared at her. 'Yeah. . .
pity. He was never right for me. We were both too
stroppy, but *you*, well, you're a very persuasive young
woman. That overpowering ex-husband of mine
doesn't know that it was you that convinced me I had
to sign the consent form. We both owe ya, Leah.'

She shook her head.

'No, you don't,' she said awkwardly. 'What I did
was a small thing. The big things were what Nathan
had to do for Bobby, and the dreadful decision that
you had forced upon you.'

The American woman sighed.

'Yeah, well, it's all over now, an' Bobby can't wait
to get his new leg. Geez! What a thought, eh?' but
she had managed a smile as she said it.

From the moment Thomas Whateley had arrived at
Barleyfields, Mabel's brother ceased to be a reluctant
visitor. In fact, he now came twice weekly, and if the
retired factory owner wasn't already seated beside his
sister, he went to seek him out.

Thomas and Mabel had become great friends. Both
intelligent and tolerant, they were very likeable people,
who found much pleasure in each other's company. It
seemed as if meeting the tranquil old lady had given
Thomas a new lease of life. He was eating better,
feeling better, even putting on a little weight, and all
because he was happy.

When the staff teased Mabel about her boyfriend,

she would laugh and tell them it was too bad she had had to wait until she was turned ninety before a man looked at her. On one occasion she had confided to Suzie, on a more sober note, but without malice, that her brother had made sure that any men friends got a cold reception because *he* wanted her full attention.

'Our parents died when I was in my early teens,' she had said, 'and because I was the eldest I automatically took over running the house and looking after Rupert. Once he realised he was on to a good thing, he made sure I kept on with it.'

'Has he never married?' the young care assistant had asked, and had been told with Mabel's usual chuckle, 'Naw. Nobody would have him.'

When Rupert visited, he made no bones about monopolising Thomas, giving his sister scant attention, and the other man, rather than see her embarrassed, listened patiently to Rupert's ramblings about years past, with himself always at the centre of the story.

He arrived one afternoon to find his sister and Thomas, along with various others of the old folk, eating oysters, and was somewhat miffed to discover that, when Mabel had remarked that it was years since she had had oysters and could just fancy tasting them again, her wish had been granted.

To her amazement and delight, Thomas had sent for his chauffeur and instructed him not to come back without a supply of the delicacy, and so consequently, her face aglow at the unexpected treat, Mabel had been holding an 'oyster party'. For once, Rupert's old boss was not offering a listening ear to what had gone on in past years inside Whateley's stores.

'It looks as if *you're* having a better time than *I* am,' Rupert said sourly, as he claimed the chair on the other side of her. 'Maybe I ought to move in here myself.'

Mabel had swung round to face him, aghast.

'What do you mean?'

'Well, if Barleyfields is good enough for Mr Whateley, I'm sure it's good enough for me.'

Thomas had seen Mabel's alarm and he intervened briskly, 'Come now, Rupert, *you're* a fit man. What would you want in a place like this?'

'Our attention. . .day and night,' Mabel had whispered grimly. 'He'd have us pinned down with no means of escape.'

Rupert was looking around him thoughtfully, and Thomas patted her hand.

'Don't worry. I don't think he means it. Just a matter of something to say.'

'I hope you're right,' she said with a frown, the little treat having lost its sparkle.

John Sullivan was fifty-five years old and in the advanced stages of multiple sclerosis. Social Services had done as promised and speeded up the paperwork to get him transferred to Barleyfields from St Bridget's where he had been hospitalised for some time.

In his case, the damage to the myelin in the brain and spinal cord had been extensive and he was now paralysed and prone to urinary tract infections, painful spasms of the muscles, and skin ulceration among other distressing symptoms.

He had been admitted to St Bridget's with an acute flare-up of the illness after a period of remission, and had been given a course of corticosteroid drugs to combat it. Once it had subsided, his married daughter with whom he lived had felt that she could no longer cope with nursing her father at home, and had approached Social Services with the end result of John becoming a patient in Barleyfields.

When the ambulance carrying the new admission had pulled up outside, Nathan was having a quick cup of coffee in the kitchen, and as the attendants brought

John Sullivan in he came to stand in the hallway, cup in hand.

'This the Social Services transfer?' he asked.

Leah nodded as she went past, and all the time she was directing the ambulance men to a pleasant ground-floor bedroom, she could feel Nathan's speculative gaze upon her. When the sick man had been placed carefully on to an air-bed, and his immediate needs dealt with, she came out of the room to find him still there.

'Were you wanting a word with Mr Sullivan?' she asked, with the cool impersonality that was now her manner towards him.

There had been little conversation between them since the day Terry had disrupted her life again, and what there had been was strictly professional. *He* didn't call her 'Leah, darling' any more, and *she* was managing to stop herself from melting every time she saw him by keeping herself under a tight control.

'Er, no, not at this moment. He'll be exhausted with the transfer from Bridget's. I'll introduce myself tomorrow.'

'So was there something else?'

She was still cool, still aloof, so why were her cheeks burning?

Eyes blue as the summer sky, the enticing slenderness of her enhancing the neat blue uniform, and the ebony waves swept back with a silver comb, she was back to her normal good health. . .physically. Mentally she was far from healed, and the man eyeing her thoughtfully from just a few feet away was the cause of it.

'Yes, as a matter of fact there is,' he said edgily. 'I've been wanting to discuss a serious matter with you.'

Leah tensed. What was coming now? More censure? She stared at him glacially and he hesitated, then sighed and lowered his eyes. She braced herself for what was coming. Without lifting his head he asked, 'What about this carpet? Do you think it needs cleaning?'

A question so completely mundane was the last thing she had been expecting and she found herself swallowing back frustrated tears.

CHAPTER NINE

ON A warm morning in early June, Leah was settling
Jack and a much frailer Jean into sun-loungers on the
back patio when Nathan came striding across from the
bungalow.

It had been one of those days when everything had
gone wrong. The milkman had been late, one of the
staff had accidentally knocked over a large plant at
the top of the stairs and there had been soil everywhere. Then Mary, who was now back after her hip
repair, had managed to get into one of the bathrooms,
with rather damp consequences. The result was that
Leah was feeling somewhat frayed, and the sight of
her employer zooming up in a crisp cream shirt and
immaculate brown trousers, with the sun glinting on
the dark russet of his hair, and his skin glowing gold
with the beginning of a tan, made her feel hot and
crumpled.

'Ah! There you are,' he observed smoothly. 'Everything all right?'

Leah sighed. She was not going to recite a catalogue
of the day's small gripes and catastrophies, not to
Nathan, who had his doubts about her capabilities, and
so she said, 'Yes, fine, thank you.'

He smiled, and as always her eyes went to his lips.

'Good. I have a message for you from Bobby.'

She pushed a strand of dark hair off her forehead
and found herself returning the smile.

'Oh, yes? What is it?'

'Katie and yourself are invited to a "leg party".'

Her mouth rounded into a small 'o' of surprise and
amusement warmed her eyes.

'Really?'

He nodded.

'Yes. He's about to discard the temporary prosthesis. The one I've had specially made for him is ready. They've taken a mould from the stump and I'm expecting the socket to be a first-class fit, and the extensions to look as natural as possible. Hopefully he'll soon be really mobile, as he's already made some progress at the walking classes. Naturally, this limb will be the first of a few. There will have to be others as he grows, but as with many things, the first one is the most important.'

Her mouth softened. It had been a gruelling time for him and it still was not over, but the pattern he had mapped out for Bobby was falling into place. Although the boy was having to face the unpleasant effects of chemotherapy, the invitation to a 'leg party' proved that he was taking it all in his stride, or what was left of it.

'Tell him that we're delighted to accept,' she told Nathan easily, the constraint between them momentarily forgotten. 'And am I to take it that it's an occasion to bring a sock rather than a bottle?'

He grinned.

'Yes, something like that. He'll be pleased to see you both.'

'When is it?' she asked.

'Friday night.'

'And then?'

'Once he's got used to it, they're going back to London. The chemotherapy will be administered there and he'll attend a limb clinic in the area.'

'You'll miss him,' she said softly.

He was sombre now.

'Yes, I certainly will, but I shall go to visit. Maxine and I are on better terms these days.'

Suddenly the sun wasn't so bright. On better terms,

were they? Was Nathan still in love with his cool American wife? After all, it wasn't *he* who had wanted the divorce, and the criticism *had* been all on her side.

She bent to rearrange the cushions behind Jean and said without looking up, 'So some good *has* come out of all this.'

The sombre mood was still on him, and as she didn't offer to raise her eyes he said stiffly, 'Yes. . .some,' and went on his way.

On Friday night, Leah dressed with extreme care. It would be the first time she and Nathan had met socially since the breakdown in communications, and even though she was constantly telling herself that their brief attraction was over, it didn't mean that she wanted him to see her as anything less than desirable. So, allowing vanity to triumph, she chose a dress of coral silk that clung to her breasts and waist and flared around her slender legs. High-heeled black shoes and a short black jacket completed the ensemble, and her mother's pearls with matching ear loops glowed milkily against the vivid fabric.

As she was observing herself in front of the mirror, Katie came up from behind, and in an outfit of a sloppy white top and tight black leggings that contrasted sharply with Leah's elegance, she asked, 'Is all this for Nathan Bonner?'

Leah's laugh was not as convincing as she would have liked.

'No, of course not. It's in Bobby's honour. *He* will have all his father's attention tonight. . .and you must remember that wearing a uniform all the time can be very restricting.'

'Yes, I believe you,' Katie said with wicked solemnity, and they both began to laugh, but Katie was quickly serious again.

'I've worked it out that if you marry Mr Bonner,

Bobby will be my stepnephew, and I'm not sure that I like the idea.'

Leah swung round to confront her and, managing to keep a straight face, asked, 'Why not?'

'Well, I don't think I'd be allowed to marry my stepnephew.'

She reached out and patted Katie's fair head.

'Don't you think we're getting into the realms of fantasy, my poppet,' she said gently. 'To begin with *I'm* not going to marry anybody, and if by any remote chance I *did* change my mind, it won't be to someone who disapproves of me as much as Nathan does. So there's no cause for you to start worrying about getting a special dispensation to marry your stepnephew!'

Katie wasn't entirely convinced.

'All right, if you say so, but I've seen Bobby's dad looking at you and he goes all smouldery.'

'That's irritation, not unrequited passion,' Leah told her with feigned nonchalance, and on that dismissive note she led the way to the car.

There seemed to be a lot of people in Bobby's room when they got to the hospital, but in fact it was only Nathan, Maxine and Dex, a junior doctor, and a couple of nurses.

'Hi, Katie!' Bobby cried excitedly as they hesitated in the doorway, and at the sound of his greeting Nathan looked up and their eyes held; *her* blue gaze was guarded and unreadable, and in *his* bright brown glance there was approval, and with it the faintest trace of indecision. But surely that couldn't be what it was. In anybody else, maybe, but not Nathan Bonner.

'Howdy! C'mon in,' Maxine called from across the room, and as Katie went to Bobby's side like a bird to its nest, Nathan strolled across to Leah.

'You look very beautiful, Leah Morgan,' he said in a low voice and in the same tone he might have used to tell her there was a smut on her nose. 'But then you *are* very beautiful. Who is it that you're dressed up for?'

Leah flinched. He could hurt her as no one else on earth.

'Bobby, of course, who else?'

'I thought you were perhaps meeting your light-fingered friend afterwards.'

Her heart twisted. He hadn't forgotten seeing her in Terry's arms all those weeks ago. I hate you, Nathan, she thought tearfully, knowing that she had already decided that hate was akin to love.

She braced herself to fight back.

'Why not? At least Terry isn't criticising me all the time!'

But then he wouldn't be, would he? He was out of her life. . .permanently, but there was no way she was going to vouchsafe that information to the Grand Inquisitor who was eyeing her stonily from just a foot away.

Maxine appeared at his side, and, laying a proprietiorial hand on his arm, she drawled, 'C'mon, honey. Bobby's waitin' for the leg show.'

'Yes, of course, I'm coming,' he said tonelessly, and for a second, Leah thought that his face was thinner and the zest gone out of him. Where Maxine had seemed to be the more fraught of the two, she was now the more relaxed one, and Leah wondered why.

Surely Nathan must be relieved that he had been given the chance to operate on Bobby and the surgery was now over, she reasoned. All right, there was still the chemotherapy to come and it was never pleasant, but it was an added precaution that would make Bobby's chances of survival much better than they would have been at one time.

Watching Nathan, she saw that he had thrown off whatever was bugging him and with his usual aplomb was gesturing towards Bobby, who was seated on a high straight-backed chair nearby.

'Bobby has invited us here to christen his new leg,' he said crisply, 'but before we do so, he's going to give us a preview. Isn't that right?' he asked of his son.

'Sure is,' the boy said, with his ready smile, and, raising himself up with the arms of the chair, he stood upright, wobbling slightly, but on two feet.

When the nurses hurried forward to assist him, he waved them back and hitched up his trouser leg to display the plastic socket neatly suctioned to the stump, and below it the inner struts of the extensions which had been filled out with foam rubber to match the shape of the missing leg and then covered in leather.

He smiled at the tense faces around him.

'I'm gonna call it Arty,' he announced.

'Why Arty?' Katie asked.

He grinned. 'You know. . .artificial.'

She laughed and the others joined in, and as the atmosphere lightened, he moved forward slowly, and laboriously made his way round the room, to be greeted with a cheer as he eased himself back into the chair.

As champagne corks popped and savouries and sweet pastries were passed amongst them, Leah found Dexter Schultz at her side. As she looked up at the amiable Texan he said, 'Sure do appreciate what you did in persuadin' Maxie to give consent. I don't doubt she *would* have done in the end, but it needed a shove in the right direction, and you were just the person to give it, young lady. She's mighty sorry about the way she treated Nathan all those years ago, knows it was all her fault, but she's trod a different path since then, an' so has he. We thought, Maxie and me, that mebbe *you* were walkin' Nathan's way.' He cocked an enquiring eyebrow. 'We'd be mighty pleased if you were.'

Leah was aware that Nathan was watching them

from across the room and she was hoping that he could not hear what Dexter was saying, but then, if he could, he would hear her reply.

She managed to conjure up an enigmatic smile and said, 'I'm afraid I have to disappoint you, Dex. Far from walking the same way, I'd say that Nathan and I are going in opposite directions.' And if the man in question could hear what they were saying, he could put that in his pipe and smoke it, she thought grimly.

It appeared that he was not listening. Annette Pryce had appeared out of nowhere, looking extremely smart in a dark green suit that set off the flame of her hair, and she was hanging on to his arm like a limpet.

An hour went by and Leah felt she had had enough. Nathan seemed to be absorbed in the late arrival, Maxine and Dex along with Katie were hovering around Bobby, the hospital staff had made themselves scarce for the time being, and she was alone and feeling more depressed by the minute.

When she whispered in Katie's ear that she was ready to go, there was no agreement from her young sister.

'*I* don't want to go yet!' she protested.

'Well, *I* do!' Leah hissed, knowing that if she had to watch Annette smarming up to Nathan for a minute longer she would explode.

Incredibly, he must have guessed what they were saying and Leah found him by her side saying silkily, 'If you have a more pressing engagement, I'll drive Katie home.'

Leah glared at him. If she *did* have any plans for later, it would only be a lonely supper after Katie was asleep, followed by what was bound to be a restless night in her solitary single bed.

'Katie is *my* responsibility,' she told him tight-lipped. '*I* brought her, and *I'm* taking her back.'

He was eyeing the beautiful dress again, and she

said in reckless anger. 'I put it on for *you*, Nathan, though I don't know why. You've already described me as beautiful, but for some reason it's never seemed like a compliment. Even if it was, it hasn't helped me to break through the barrier of your disdain, as you also find me inept. . .and stupid, too, with regard to what you see as my spineless resurge of affection for Terry. Dexter has just been telling me that Maxine blames herself for what happened all those years ago, but if you were as high-handed and arrogant then as you are now, I'm not so sure!'

They were standing near the open doorway, and with a quick look around to make sure they weren't being observed, Nathan gripped her wrist and whisked her outside into the corridor.

His hand was warm and vibrant on her skin and, as before, his touch sparked off the dangerous flame.

'High-handed and arrogant, am I?' he said in a harsh whisper. 'And what about you? You're encased in ice. All pleasant and punctilious inside Barleyfields, but for the rest of the time completely out of reach. Well, here's a little something to thaw you out,' and he kissed her long and savagely, to the amazement of a couple of women cleaners who were apathetically propelling their polishing machines along the corridor.

When he released her, Leah swayed on her feet and his hand came out to steady her. As she gazed at him, speechless, he said, 'Any time you want another dose of the treatment let me know, but don't expect it to be slotted in along with your criminal friend's requirements.'

Tears thickened her throat. His kiss had shaken her with its ferocity, yet she had still responded, still melted at the contact, and now he was being flippant again. Why, for heaven's sake, was she not putting him right about Terry and clearing the air between them?

Katie's voice broke into the confused maelstrom of her thoughts.

'I'm ready to go if you wish, Leah,' she said from the doorway. 'Bobby's tired. His mum thinks he needs to rest.'

Leah dragged her mind out of its turbulent channels and tuned in to what Katie was saying, aware that Nathan's burning gaze was still on her.

'Er. . .yes. . .all right, Katie. I'm ready when you are, but first I must say goodbye to everyone, and I just want one more word with Bobby's dad, if you'll excuse me.'

Katie's eyes lingered on both their faces for a second and then she said easily, 'Yes, sure, Leah.'

As she opened her mouth to speak, Leah knew that pride was not going to allow her to tell him that Terry *was* out of her life. She was about to make matters worse, and as if driven by some inner craving for pain she said, 'Regarding the treatment, I think the one dose was enough. I shan't be asking for a repeat prescription.' And before he could answer, she'd gone inside to join the others.

After a long, miserable weekend that had only been lightened by Katie's cheerful presence, Monday morning and Barleyfields came as a grateful return to normality, but even there gloom was to be found.

When the report from over the weekend was read, Leah was surprised to find that Mabel Curtis was off her food. She had not had a bite since Saturday morning, which was most unusual as she had a hearty appetite, and she immediately went to check if the old lady was sickening for something.

'What's wrong, Mabel?' she asked when she found her sitting listlessly in the front lounge, hands idle in her lap, her crocheting nowhere to be seen.

Mabel looked up and Leah was shocked to see how

the life seemed to have gone out of her.

'It's Rupert,' she said.

'Your brother!' Leah exclaimed. 'What is it? Is he ill?'

Mabel shook her head. 'Naw, I might feel better about it if he were.'

'I'm not with you,' Leah said, puzzled.

'He came to see me on Saturday morning and announced that he wants to move in here. Reckons it's to be near me, but it's Thomas that's the attraction.' Her voice broke. 'I don't want him here, Sister. I thought I'd finally managed to get away from him and now he's coming back into my life. He'll be bossing and manipulating me again. I won't have a minute's peace.'

Leah frowned. 'Does Thomas know?'

'No. His nephew came to pick him up on Saturday morning and he's staying with him all over the weekend. He's due back this afternoon.'

'I see. Well, Rupert can't come into Barleyfields at the moment as we haven't got a vacant room,' Leah consoled her.

'Yes, I know,' Mabel agreed sombrely, 'but the moment you have he'll be in.' She shook her head. 'I can't understand it. He's fit and well, and wouldn't have touched this place with a bargepole if Thomas hadn't been here.'

'I suppose we could keep fobbing him off,' Leah suggested thoughtfully, 'as he's not ill; but I would have to consult Nathan first.'

'No, don't do that, Sister,' she said. 'If he wants to come in and there's a vacancy, let him. God only knows I don't want him here, but neither do I want to meet my maker with any guilt inside of me.'

Leah patted her hand.

'Forget it for now, Mabel. Let's worry about it when we have a room free, eh?'

'Aye, I suppose so,' she agreed mournfully. 'But we

both know how quickly things change in these sorts of places, don't we? Maybe he'll be able to have mine.'

'Now that's enough, Mabel,' Leah chided gently. 'I'm going to ask Suzie to bring your breakfast, and I want you to promise me you'll eat it.'

The old lady managed a smile.

'I'll try, but I feel as if it'll choke me.'

Whenever Nathan wasn't around Leah found herself listening for his footsteps, but he didn't appear, and her mind kept going back to the fiasco of their last meeting.

Had he gone back to the so obvious attentions of Annette Pryce after they had left, she wondered, passing off what had happened on the corridor as putting a member of staff in her place. But it was hardly to do with their employer/employee relationship, was it? It was a case of an attractive worldly man and a wary and vulnerable woman fighting their way through a jungle of sexual chemistry and conflicting personalities, and she told herself if she didn't put the memory of that savage kiss out of her mind, she was going to be good for nothing for the rest of the day.

Gordon Bell popped in during the early afternoon with the suggestion that she and Katie should make their proposed visit to his home the following day and, having an engagement book that was ominously empty, she accepted. It would be somewhere to go, something to do, providing Katie had not made other arrangements.

She had.

'I can't come,' she said, with a noticeable lack of regret. 'We've got a maths test on Wednesday and as I'm behind in my schoolwork with being in Canada, I haven't a hope of passing unless I study beforehand.'

'That's all right. I'll go on my own,' Leah offered, 'but promise me that you'll get a friend to come and study with you so that I won't be leaving you alone.'

'Yes, OK,' she agreed, and so it transpired that Leah was alone when she arrived at the smart detached house less than a mile away.

As she had been easing her car down the drive at Barleyfields, Nathan's Jaguar had passed her and they had exchanged cool nods, each making a quick appraisal of the other, and in his case, eyebrows lifting as he saw that she was wearing the same dress she had worn for Bobby's party.

It had been a deliberate choice, though she doubted anyone else would understand the mechanics of it. By wearing it at the Bells', it would cease to be of any particular importance in her wardrobe and, hopefully, any future memories it might evoke would be of a happy young family rather than a disturbing ortho- paedic surgeon.

Gordon Bell had not exaggerated about his family. His wife, Gaynor, was a friendly attractive brunette, and his daughter an entrancing one-year-old with her father's dark colouring, called Lucinda.

He had just got back from evening surgery when she arrived. and as he poured her a sherry, with his little girl gurgling nearby, and his wife busying herself in the kitchen, Leah felt a pain around her heart and knew it to be envy. For a brief unbidden second she had a vision of Nathan and herself in a house of their own, with a sweet-faced baby to adore, and longing tore at her.

'You all right, Leah?' her host asked as she sipped the amber liquid.

'Er—yes. . .why?'

'Just thought you looked a bit peaky. Not Bonner, is it?'

She stared at him, her colour rising.

'What do you mean?'

'Throwing his weight about.'

'No, of course not,' she said in immediate defence of him. 'I have the greatest respect for Nathan Bonner. He's just had a horrendous family crisis to deal with and never batted an eyelid.'

'You mean having to operate on his kid?'

'So you know about it?'

'Of course. We medics have our grapevine, just like anybody else. The lad should congratulate himself on having a father who's the best in his field.'

He was beginning to irritate her.

'And should he also congratulate himself on losing a leg?' she asked drily.

He shrugged.

'He's likely to live, and that's more than a lot of cancer patients can hope for.'

'You sound very sure of it.'

'Well, let's put it this way. He'll have a damn good chance, and Bonner's certain to follow it up with chemo, and while we're on the subject of your employer, I'm told he has a rich American wife.'

'Ex-wife,' she corrected quickly.

'OK. Ex-wife, then. Somebody was telling me that up to this happening, he'd hardly seen the kid in years.'

'That's not been *his* fault,' she snapped, and he looked at her in surprise.

'Oh! So Bonner's got himself a champion,' he said with a grating laugh.

'Not exactly,' she said stiffly, wondering what on earth had possessed her to get involved in this conversation, 'but I *do* like to give credit where it's due.'

'If you fancy him you won't be the only one, Leah,' he said, with a patronising smile. 'He's had plenty after him, but. . .'

She had to ask. 'But what?'

'But none of them got anywhere, as far as I know. He's too choosy.'

'I see. Well, I suppose it's better than jumping into

bed with everyone on offer,' she said smoothly, aware that she was still defending Nathan. That proved to be the end of the conversation as at that moment Gaynor came in to say that the meal was ready.

She seated Leah at the far end of the table from where her young daughter was spooning puréed meat and vegetables into her mouth with only average accuracy.

'I'm putting you out of aiming distance,' she said laughingly, 'as Lucinda isn't fussy where she throws her food when she gets fed up.'

'She's an adorable little girl,' Leah said with the ache in her heart again.

'*We* think so, don't we, darling?' the doting father said, and his wife nodded proudly.

It was a pleasant enough evening, the meal enjoyable, her hostess a friendly uncomplicated girl, and the chubby Lucinda a joy to watch as she splashed around in the bath, but the conversation with Gordon had taken the edge off it. His manner while discussing Nathan had been condescending and rather spiteful, and as she drove home after saying her goodbyes at the earliest opportunity, Leah was aware that the young GP was curious about Nathan and herself. He sensed a situation and, given the chance, wouldn't hesitate to tittle tattle around until his curiosity was satisfied, she thought angrily.

She had to smile, though. *She* was allowed to criticise Nathan, but she wasn't prepared to stand by and let anyone else do so. That resolve persisted until she entered the flat and discovered from Katie and her friend Vicky that they had had a visitor.

'Mr Bonner's been round while you were out,' her young sister said, looking up from her books.

'Oh? What did he want?'

'He saw the light on and came to check that I was all right. I introduced him to Vicky.'

Leah stiffened. He really was the limit! The next thing she knew, he would be having the NSPCC round!

Katie's friend giggled.

'Isn't he brill! He looks like Harrison Ford.'

'I suppose he wanted to know where I was,' Leah said tetchily.

Katie's smile was guileless. 'But of course. It was *you* he'd come to see.'

'No, it wasn't,' she snapped. 'He saw me going out.'

'Well, whatever. I told him you were dining with one of the doctors who comes to the home.'

'And did you also tell him that the man has a wife and child?'

'Why, no,' Katie said innocently. 'Has he?'

Leah advanced on her threateningly.

'Now look here, young lady. . .' and as Katie pretended to cower, she said briskly, 'Come on, you've both studied long enough. Go and get in the car and we'll take Vicky home.'

As the days went by, Mabel's depression deepened, and to a lesser degree it was shared by Thomas Whateley. Each time Rupert came to visit, he stressed his intention of moving into Barleyfields at the first opportunity, and matters were not improved by his waylaying Nathan, who hadn't yet been told of the situation, and being assured by him that the first vacancy would be his.

When Leah had expressed her dismay at the turn of events, Nathan said angrily, 'If you'd taken the trouble to put me in the picture, I would have known how to handle his request, but as you didn't, I told him what I would have told anyone wanting to move in. After all, the man *does* have a heart complaint.'

Leah stared at him in surprise. 'I wasn't aware of it, and I'm sure Mabel isn't.'

'No? Well, according to him, he has.'

'With regard to my not informing you of Rupert Curtis's intentions,' she said stiffly, aware that she was being put in the wrong again, 'there hasn't been any necessity for mentioning it until a room becomes vacant. If that had occurred, I would have consulted you immediately.'

'What you're really saying is that if you can avoid talking to me you will,' he said drily. 'That's fine by me, but you might just do it once too often. Communication is a very important part of the job here. On the other hand, there might come a day when you'll be desperate to speak to me and I won't be available, but that's the other side of the coin.'

She went weak with dismay. 'What do you mean? That you won't be here?'

There was been a glint in his eye that she could not identify as he said, 'I'm not *chained* to this place, even though it is very dear to my heart. There'd always be someone to step into my place at St Bernadette's if I decided to go elsewhere. I have no ties, and there are some tempting openings in other parts of the world.'

Misery gripped her. How would she exist if he went away? Nathan had erupted into her life with all the force of a volcano, and even if nothing came of their relationship she would still want to be near him.

'You say you've no ties, but what about Bobby?' she protested weakly.

His face sobered.

'I've never really been in his life until now, and I'm not going to pass up the chance of getting to know my son better. You can bet on that! But Maxine and Dex won't want me forever on their doorstep.'

'So you're not still in love with her?' she asked carefully. 'When I saw you together on the night of Bobby's operation, I thought that maybe. . .'

He stared at her blankly.

'You didn't come near St Bernadette's that night.'

'No, of course I didn't,' she agreed quickly. 'It must be another occasion I'm thinking of.'

She had thrown him off balance. She could tell by his expression, but his answer to the question was definite enough.

'Of course I'm not in love with Maxine. Never in a thousand years! And some kind of wimp I'd be to carry that sort of torch all this time, especially after her finding me so unsavoury.'

Leah shook her head at that. 'Dex said she had admitted that it was all her fault.'

He sighed. 'It takes two to tango. . .and two to break up a marriage, Leah.'

And two to reach the heights of heaven, if they're right for each other, she wanted to cry, but Giles came beside her with the lunch menu in his hand, a bell was ringing in one of the upstairs rooms, and Charlie was tapping her on the arm and asking, 'When am I going to the farm? Them cows will be brimmin' over,' and in the middle of what was all in a day's work at Barleyfields, Nathan went on his way.

The following week Jean Garside had a massive stroke resulting in a left hemiplegia which caused flaccid weakness in the limbs, and her speech to become more slurred and indistinct.

When he realised what had happened, the devoted Jack became disorientated and frightened, and took to wandering around the home, wailing inconsolably.

Their GP was sent for and he prescribed a strong sedative which made Jack calm down into a state of blank numbness that was almost catatonic.

The staff were saddened to see the breaking up of the loving partnership, and as the standard treatment for cases such as Jean's was put into practice, Leah hoped that correct support while in bed, exercising under the supervision of the visiting physiotherapist, and some speech therapy if the sick woman was up to it, might bring about some improvement in her condition.

Jack's wanderings ceased, and now he was always to be found beside her bed, holding her cold limp hand and staring into space. Observing them, it was difficult to say which of the two was the more to be pitied.

Whenever Nathan came in, he made a point of visiting the subdued man and his hemiplegic wife, and on one occasion when he and Leah were in the room at the same time, he said sombrely, 'Old age is no joke, eh, Leah? We should all make the most of what life has to offer before we're too old to enjoy it.'

She eyed him warily. Was there a message in the remark for her? She doubted it, and if there was, it was *he* who was stopping her from making the most of *her* life.

She bent to straighten the covers and said quietly, 'The only comfort is that it comes to all of us if we live that long.' Her voice broke, as a vision of her mother came into mind, young, pretty. . .alive, until her alloted time had run out.

Nathan eyed her questioningly, and as she gulped back the tears, he came to stand beside her. 'What is it? What's hurting you?'

She brushed her hand across her stinging eyes. 'My mum. . .I was thinking about my mum. She was so lovely. . .so kind. She died not so very long ago.'

Nathan put his arms around her and patted the top of his dark head gently and she leaned against him, taking comfort from his nearness. There was no passion in them, just a rare moment of peace, and she wanted it to go on for ever, but Suzie was hovering in the doorway with the news that John Sullivan's daughter wanted a word with Sister about her father, and that Mabel was off her food again.

CHAPTER TEN

BOBBY went back to London, leaving Katie forlorn, and Leah with a depressing feeling that her links with Nathan were disappearing. It was his son's illness that had brought them together, and it had continued to be a source of personal contact outside of Barleyfields ever since, even though the quality of their relationship had worsened. Now her only contact with him would be the nursing home, and if he went away there wouldn't even be that. All of which was hardly creating a chirpy atmosphere in the flat.

'Bobby's promised to keep in touch,' Katie said, after their final visit, 'but it's not going to be easy, is it, Leah, him in London and me here?'

Leah had eyed her anxiously. The pangs of young love could be just as painful as those of a more mature attraction, she thought tenderly, but youthful passions came and went, and hopefully Katie wouldn't continue to pine for the plucky American boy who had come into their lives for a short time.

'No, it isn't,' she agreed, 'but if that's what he said I'm sure he must have meant it. You've helped him a lot while he's been here and I'm sure he won't forget you.'

'Do you really think so,' Katie said, her pixie face all pinched and miserable.

'Of course I do,' Leah assured her staunchly, giving her a comforting hug. 'You'll see.'

It was at this time that Leah's concern for Mabel Curtis increased. The old lady still wasn't eating and consequently was losing weight, but that wasn't worrying her the most. The physical problem could be put

163

right with gentle persuasion at meal times and extra vitamins. It was her mental state that gave the most cause for alarm. She had sunk into a mood of black depression that even Thomas could not lift.

He had sent for his chauffeur and taken her for drives in the country, which she could cope with as long as she did not have to get out of the car, but there had been no response to the outside world with its summer landscapes. Thomas had arranged for oysters to be brought in for her again, but she hadn't touched them, and so it was continuing, and all because of Rupert's determination to join her in Barleyfields.

'You'll just have to tell him straight that you don't want him here with you,' Leah suggested gently. 'The prospect is making you ill, Mabel, and we don't want that,' but she just shook her head stubbornly, and said, 'What has to be will be, Sister. I shouldn't be making all this fuss. I'm tired, and the sooner the Lord takes me the better.'

Thomas Whateley sitting nearby shook his head in disbelief.

'Is this the same woman who only a short time ago was the life and soul of Barleyfields?' he said, sadly. 'Rupert has something to answer for! It might be poking my nose in but I've a good mind to tackle him, the next time he comes to visit.'

'Do you honestly think he would know what you were on about?' Leah said. 'He's so wrapped up in himself, and Mabel is adamant that we don't pursue the matter.' So it was shelved for the time being, but not for long.

'We're going to lose her if this goes on,' Leah said grimly one morning when Suzie had brought Mabel's breakfast back untouched again. 'All because of something that could soon be put right if she'd let us.'

Nathan was aware of the problem and just as

concerned as she, but felt that Mabel's wishes regarding the matter should be respected.

'It's a tricky situation,' he said when she expressed her deep concern over the old lady's mental state. 'I'd be perfectly willing to have a word with the old boy when next he comes to see her. Tell him that his sister's health is not good and that the strain of his continual presence in the home would be too much for her, but will he take any notice, and what will she say if she finds out?'

He perched on the corner of her desk with a coffee while the discussion took place, and Leah wondered how *he* was coping with Bobby's return to London. He seemed subdued these days which was not in keeping with his usual bounce, and she thought it must have been a wrench to have found his son and then lost him again so soon. But then he *had not* lost him, had he? Bobby was only a couple of hours' drive away. Almost as if he had been reading her thoughts, he surprised her by saying, 'I'm going to London this weekend to see Bobby, and I thought that Katie and yourself might like to come along. He's really keen to see her again, and Maxine has told me to tell you they'd be delighted to have you stay with them.'

She gaped at him.

'Us go to London with you?'

His eyes flickered away from hers.

'That's the general idea, but if it's not convenient. . . or you don't want to go. . .?'

'We'd love to see Bobby,' she said quickly. 'Katie has been moping ever since he went back home.'

'That's all right, then. If you'd like to come across to my place at nine o'clock on Saturday morning?'

'Er. . .yes. . .of course,' she agreed absently, her mind already grappling with the prospect of two days in his company and whether it would result in pain or pleasure.

Katie's reaction to the idea needed no analysing. She was delighted, and Leah could not help wishing that her own response had been as simple.

On Friday afternoon she had the overpowering urge to buy something new to wear for the coming weekend, and as all was under control inside Barleyfields, and she knew that Nathan would be occupied with his private practice in the town, she decided to take a couple of hours owing to her to do some shopping.

It proved to be one of those occasions rare to womankind when everything she had in mind was on the rails, and in just over the hour she had given in to extravagance and bought designer jeans and a crisp white shirt, a linen suit in pale yellow, and a black cat-suit with a matching multicoloured silk blouse.

She was leaving the store clutching an expensive carrier bag, eyes glowing with the pleasure of making the purchases, her step light, when she stopped in mid-stride. Nathan was on the pavement outside, talking to Annette Pryce, of all people. Annette, who was supposed to be helping to hold the fort during her absence. She was holding a small white paper bag in her hand and smiling up at him, and anger and dismay ripped through Leah.

She could have stepped back into the store unseen, or absorbed herself into the crowds to get past them, but she didn't. Instead she walked up to them and said coolly, 'What are *you* doing here, Annette?'

The other woman was taken aback to see her, but not for long.

'You'd forgotten to have the prescription made up for Jean Garside,' she said sweetly, 'and I thought I'd better get it, in case she needs the tablets.'

'Did you, indeed,' Leah said icily, aware of Nathan's eyes on her. 'So you've left the home understaffed during my absence?'

Annette shrugged.

'What you're saying is that it's all right for you to go round the shops, but not me, eh? Don't blame me because you'd forgotten the prescription.'

'You *are* to blame,' Leah flung back, 'because Jean's GP rang me when he got back to his surgery to say that he'd made a mistake in the strength of the tablets, and would call back this evening to rectify it. So perhaps you'd like to go back to the chemists and ask for it back.'

'Just as you like,' she said sulkily, and then with a smile at Nathan, who had kept silent during the altercation between them, 'Bye for now.'

When she had gone Leah's anger evaporated as quickly as it had come and she said swiftly, '*I* had a couple of hours owing to me, and came to do some shopping, but Annette had no right leaving the home when I wasn't there.'

He nodded. '*You're* running the place, and you don't have to justify your actions to *me*.'

She gave an amazed laugh. 'No? You surprise me.'

His face tightened. 'Not half as much as *you* surprise *me*.' He looked around him. 'Are you in the car?'

'Yes, it's parked around the corner.'

'Right, so I'll see you in the morning, then,' and he strolled off along the pavement, head erect, shoulders set back in a well cut dark suit, a man who would be noticed wherever he went.

London was busy, noisy, and the traffic horrendous, but it was exciting too, with hundreds of tourists strolling around in the sunshine, and famous landmarks looming up around them as Nathan pointed the Jaguar towards a quiet tree-lined square where the Schultzes had rented a house.

The journey had been pleasant and uneventful, with Katie chattering to Nathan from the back seat and Leah sitting silently beside him, trying to keep awake.

She was very tired. It had been a taxing week at the home, and on top of that she wasn't sleeping, especially during last night when her mind had been too fixed on the weekend ahead.

Each time her eyelids drooped she forced them open again, annoyed with herself for being in such a sleepy state while in Nathan's company. She had felt fresh enough as they had waited in the gardens for him to get the car out, but the moment she'd settled into its enclosed space she'd started to wilt. What had made it worse was the fact that *he* was on top form, lively, good-humoured, and dressed in the tan silk shirt of the night they had met in the supermarket, with cara-mel-coloured trousers and a cream cashmere sweater, all combining to enhance his fiery colouring.

He gave her a quick sideways glance a couple of times and she met his gaze with glazed blue eyes until eventually he said, 'If you want to go to sleep, feel free to do so. Katie and I are quite capable of entertaining each other.'

She managed to perk herself up at that and assured him that she was 'fine'.

Leah had decided to travel in the new jeans and white shirt, while Katie, as usual, had favoured one of her baggy tops and the leggings, with clumsy brogues on her feet.

'You'd better take a couple of dresses just in case we go anywhere socially,' she had suggested as she packed an overnight case, and Katie had groaned.

'Never mind the groans,' she had chided. 'I want you to look like a pretty young girl once in a while, instead of a top-heavy spider.' But Leah's smile had taken the sting out of her words, and dresses for Katie had been packed along with Leah's own new pur-chases.

In the end she closed her eyes and gave in to drowsi-ness, reasoning that it was better to be lethargic now than when they arrived at their destination, and, with the murmur of their voices going over her head, she slept until the noise of the traffic on the outskirts of London brought her into wakefulness.

'Feel better?' Nathan asked as she stretched and rubbed her eyes.

'No. I feel crumpled and my mouth is dry,' she said crustily.

'There's a flask and sandwiches in the boot,' he told her easily. 'We'll stop at the next lay-by.'

The coffee was hot and fragrant, the sandwiches delicious, but Leah would have enjoyed them more if they had been her idea instead of his. Why was it that he always made her feel so inept? Maybe it was because she was. If he had called last night and asked *her* to make the sandwiches, her best offer would have been a pallid jar of potted meat, instead of fresh salmon and succulent ham.

Bobby was feeling nauseous and had a very sore mouth, but his pleasure at seeing them was evident, and as Leah watched Nathan taking stock of his son a lump came into her throat. The keen eyes were assessing him, taking in his pallor, the obvious tenderness of his mouth. . .and his skilful handling of the leg. As Bobby and Katie went off to catch up on their news, he said to Maxine, 'The nausea and mouth ulcers are from the Methotrexate that he's on, along with the injections of Doxorubicin. These side-effects are unpleasant, but they won't last. Once the chemotherapy is over, Bobby will feel much better.' He turned to Leah. 'He seems to be handling the leg well, don't you think?'

She smiled. 'He's marvellous in every way. You must be proud of him, Maxine.'

The American woman returned her smile.

'Sure am. I wish my daddy could have lived to see

how he's coping with this, but, come on, folks, there's a meal waitin'. Dex'll be in later. He had to go into the office for a couple of hours.'

A hot lunch was ready to be served in an elegant panelled dining-room with a young maid in attendance, and as they took their seats Katie's eyes were like saucers.

Bobby grinned across at her. 'We eat in the kitchen back home.' His glance went to the maid. 'Lucy was included in the rental.'

Katie smiled back. 'You *do*? So do we,' and, reassured, she began to eat.

Leah found herself meeting Nathan's clear gaze and he raised his eyebrows whimsically as if to say, And what do *you* think about all this?

She thought that Bobby was consciously making Katie feel at ease. She also thought that, with regard to the house, it would not occur to Maxine to accept anything less than the best. That had already been proved by her insistence that Nathan should treat their son, and her final thought was that with Nathan *she* could be happy in a palace or a shack. Houses were merely bricks and mortar. It was those who lived inside them that made the home. Leah was not aware of it, but there was an appeal in her answering glance. *She* needed reassurance just as much as Katie, but from another person and for another reason.

Dex came home, and in the afternoon she and Katie sat with him on the patio at the back of the house, facing a huge flower-filled garden, while Nathan, with Maxine in attendance, took Bobby upstairs to check him over.

Once he decided that there were no problems with the stump and that 'Arty' was working fine, they came down to join them.

'Bobby will need to have a CT scan in a month or so,' Nathan told Maxine and Dex. 'To make sure that the leg is now clear, and to check on the lesions in the lungs. I'll be in touch with my counterpart at this end all along the line, so you needn't worry.'

'Yeah. You do that,' Maxine told him with the air of a woman who was used to being obeyed, and his face closed up, causing Leah to think angrily, Can't she see what he's been through, and is still going through?

But the moment passed, and on its heels Dex said jovially, 'Hear you have a birthday tomorrow, Nathan. What say we celebrate it tonight, huh?'

'We can't, honey,' his wife butted in. 'We're going to have to leave these folks while we go to Heathrow to pick up your overseas visitors. Dex has some business associates flyin' in tonight, and we've promised to pick 'em up and take 'em to their hotel,' she explained, in her nasal drawl.

Leah listened in dismay. It was Nathan's birthday tomorrow and he had never said. But then he wouldn't, would he? He probably expected her to have guessed, or looked into her crystal ball!

'I'm not too bothered about celebrating,' he said unsmilingly. 'I'll settle for a game of Scrabble with Katie and Bobby. . .and Leah, if she feels like joining in.'

'Why not?' she said brightly, aware that the way she had been tagged on at the end of the suggestion appeared to be her role in his life. . .as an after-thought.

But as they played the game in a light-hearted mood, with Nathan blatantly cheating, and Bobby and Katie howling with laughter at his mutilation of the English language, Leah relaxed, content to be there with them. . .with Nathan for a whole weekend. She thought gratefully that if it continued like this, at least there would be peace between them, if nothing else.

By ten o'clock Bobby looked as if he had had enough, and when he said he was going to bed Katie

lost interest and said she would do the same. They
foraged for milk and biscuits in the kitchen and off
they went, with Nathan eyeing Bobby in concern and
making an excuse to accompany him.

Leah went outside into the gardens. The huge bright
ball of the sun was now an amber smudge on the
horizon, and as she wandered among the flower-filled
terraces in the summer dusk she heard Nathan's footsteps coming towards her on the flagged path.

She turned quickly, the black cat-suit melting into
the gathering darkness, and only her face with its
anxious blue eyes and the vibrant colours of the blouse
were visible.

'Is Bobby all right?' she asked quickly.

'He's tired and not feeling too clever,' he replied.
'I went to make sure he could cope with undressing
and the removal of the prosthesis, but I needn't have
concerned myself. He's a very self-sufficient
young man.'

'Like his father.'

The words were out before she could stop them,
and he took a step nearer.

'Why do I have the feeling that remark wasn't meant
to be complimentary,' he said, straining to see her face.

'It *was*,' she assured him with a nervous laugh, wishing she had kept her mouth shut. 'I envy you your
self-sufficiency.'

He was only an arm's length away, and now it was
she who was straining to see *his* face.

'I'm only like that some of the time,' he said, with
a ragged laugh. 'There's a part of me that's unsure,
stumbling around in confusion, bungling everything I
do, and one person alone is responsible for that.'

Leah was staring at him open-mouthed. Did he mean
who she hoped he meant? There was a simple way to
find out.

'And who is that?'

His voice roughened.

'For God's sake; Leah, don't pretend you don't know!' he said, with such force that she took a step back.

It was an involuntary movement and she regretted it, as she stepped into nothing. There was a void beneath her feet and she was falling into it.

When Leah saw the drop afterwards in the light of day, it was only about six feet, but in the warm darkness she seemed to be falling forever, and when she *did* hit the ground, the breath was knocked out of her.

'Leah! Where are you, for God's sake?' she heard him cry in horror, and then there was a thud as he landed beside her.

'I don't know,' she gasped weakly. 'I seem to have landed on grass.'

'You must have been standing on the edge of one of the terraces. The folks who own the house should have a garden as steep as this illuminated,' he said angrily as he bent over her. 'But never mind that for the moment. Can you move everything? Back? Arms? Legs?'

Leah flexed her body slowly.

'Yes, I think so.'

'Good.' He got to his feet and peered into the darkness. 'I can make out a flight of steps just a few feet away, which I imagine will take us back to the level we were on, so hold tight my love,' and he bent and lifted her carefully into his arms.

'You're shaking,' he said gently, as he moved carefully up the steps and on to the path that led to the house, 'and no wonder after a fall like that. It could have caused untold damage.' His grip on her tightened. 'The thought of anything happening to you makes me go cold.'

She stared up at him wide eyed. Had she knocked her head and was hallucinating? But he went on as if his last remark was general comment, and told her, 'I'm prescribing a cup of hot sweet tea and a leisurely bath to take away the bruising. If there's any witch-hazel on the premises, I'll dab it on to any sore spots for you first.'

Leah nodded meekly with her face nuzzled against his chest, and her heart pounding, not just from the shock of the fall, but from his intoxicating nearness and the magical words he had just uttered.

'I'm taking you to *my* room to check you over,' he murmured against her hair, when they got back to the house. 'We can't disturb a sleeping Katie.'

Leah looked up at him. 'You can put me down, Nathan. I think I can walk.'

He gave a quirky smile.

'What's the matter? Aren't you comfortable?'

'Yes, of course,' and that was the understatement of the year! 'But I wouldn't want you to get a hernia on my account,' she said, with a shaky laugh.

His laughter was confident. . .deep in his throat.

'I'll risk a hernia for the chance to hold the Scarlet Pimpernel of Barleyfields in my arms.'

'Huh?' She wasn't with him.

'The lady who is so elusive and hard to pin down,' he explained as he climbed the wide staircase.

'That's only because she's been nervous of putting a foot wrong with the all-powerful Robespierre,' she flashed back.

His good humour was unquenchable.

'I don't recall going around spouting that any institution which does not suppose the people to be good, and the magistrates corruptible, is evil,' he said with a grin, 'and in any case that's rubbish. You had me dazzled from the start.'

He was pushing the bedroom door open with his elbow, then standing her carefully on to her feet, and eyeing her with a concerned frown, he said, 'Now. . .

do you still feel as if you're all in one piece. . .albeit a rather muddy one?'

'Yes,' she mumbled, thinking that this wasn't how she had imagined a bedroom scene with Nathan. 'The only part that feels sore is my right shoulder. I must have landed on it, I think.'

She was mortified to find that her voice was thickening with treacherous tears, but if he noticed, he didn't comment.

'Right. I'll go and see what I can find in the bathroom cabinet. I suppose it's too much to expect that people who haven't the gumption to make their garden safe would have a bottle of witch-hazel on the shelf. While I'm gone, Leah, take your blouse off and I'll examine your shoulder,' and he whisked out of the room with his purposeful stride.

Leah eased her shoulders out of the cat-suit and slowly undid the buttons of the blouse, thinking as she did so that in other circumstances there would have been something tender and precious in undressing for the man she loved, while here she was with grass in her hair, mud on her face and clothes, and an aching shoulder!

When he came back, Nathan was holding aloft a brown bottle and exclaiming, 'Bingo! Maxine's absent landlords have redeemed themselves.'

His eyes went to the graceful stem of her neck, the smooth shoulders beneath it, and the soft breasts in her best wispy lace, and Leah thought that they darkened. But first and foremost he was the doctor—the orthopaedic surgeon—and as his pliant hands explored her shoulder, he said 'Everything seems to be in place. The scapula is intact; you haven't broken the clavicle, as you're moving your arm normally from the socket, and there's no sagging of the limb.'

He picked up the bottle and poured some of the age-old remedy into the palm of his hand.

'You'll no doubt have used this before, Leah,' he said. 'It feels very cold when first on the skin, but it should take away the pain and bruising, and then, in a few moments, take that bath, eh?'

She nodded, aware that Nathan was doing all the talking. . .that *she* had hardly spoken since entering the room, so mesmerised was she by the fall and the situation that had developed from it. As if aware of her silence, he took a step back to observe her. What he saw was beautiful blue eyes meeting his, ivory skin covered in wispy lace, and his eyes went to the bed with its pristine sheets.

'I've never ravished a patient yet,' he said with a teasing smile, 'but I might be tempted if you were in a fitter state, my darling.'

At his words, the blood in her veins became desire, sweet joyful desire, and music played in her heart. Her aches and pains forgotten, she held out her hands to him, and as he took them in his and pulled her to him there was a fire in him to match her own, but it seemed that *his* feet were still firmly on the ground.

'Go and have your bath, Leah,' he said softly, kissing the tip of her muddy nose. 'There'll be another day. . .another time. . .all the rest of our lives, in fact.'

She touched his cheek gently. He was everything she had ever wanted, and her smile dazzled him with its brilliance.

'You're right, of course, Nathan,' she said softly, her eyes on the lips that promised paradise. Her laugh was low and happy. 'But then, you always are.'

'Not always.' He was releasing her. 'I've told you how you affect me.'

She laughed again. 'Yes. . .and I don't believe it.'

'You have to, because it's true.' He gave her a gentle push towards the door. 'Go straight to bed after the bath. . .doctor's orders. . .and *I'll* wait up for Maxine and Dex.'

Leah pulled a face at him from the doorway. 'Do I *have* to go to bed?'

'Yes, you do. . .and. . .'

'Yes?' she breathed.

'I'll see you in the morning, my love.'

CHAPTER ELEVEN

NATHAN's birthday started off on the right note, with
his son feeling better after a night's sleep and pre-
senting him with a card from Bobby and Arty, along
with a book of poems by Beryl Shill, a Gloucester poet.

Leah watched his pleasure as he accepted the gift
and was surprised that the haunting magic of the
diminutive woman's words should appeal to someone
as positive as he.

She would have been miserable having no gift for
him if he hadn't murmured in her ear as they sat down
to breakfast. 'Your gift is appreciated just as much.'

'But *I* haven't given you anything,' she said awkwardly.

He smiled. 'You have. Your presence. . .your
being here.'

She'd smiled her brilliant smile, eyes aglow. The
unbelievable was happening. It was all going to
come right.

Maxine and Dex took them out to lunch and the
atmosphere was relaxed and carefree because they
were all together and Bobby was having a good day.
The hours passed in a happy haze with the young ones
in high spirits, the Schultzes looking on indulgently,
and Nathan and Leah tantalisingly aware of each other.

'Promise you'll come again, Katie,' the boy said
when they were ready for off, and she turned to
Nathan.

'Can we?'

He smiled. 'I don't see why not,' and to Maxine and
Dex, 'If there's anything worrying you at any time,
ring me. . .day or night. I see no cause for alarm with

regard to Bobby at the moment, and if I've done my part right, the scan in a couple of weeks' time should show that the leg is clear and we've only the lungs to worry about.'

They left London in the early evening and though they had not managed any time alone. . .had not even touched. . .each time their eyes met, joy bells rang in Leah's heart.

Katie was the one who was subdued this time. She had little to say and spent the time gazing at the pop magazines Bobby had given her.

They were on the last few miles when the phone on the dashboard rang and Nathan groaned. 'I'm supposed to be incommunicado,' he said as he switched into the call.

Watching him, Leah saw his face stretch into a smile as he exclaimed, 'Jules! Hello! What can I do for you, *mon ami*?'

There was silence as he listened to what the caller had to say. His face was grave. 'Hurler's Syndrome. . . gargoylism? What age is the child?' He tutted thoughtfully. 'Know what to look for, do you? Cardiac abnormalities, enlarged tongue, liver, spleen, umbilical hernia.'

There was another pause and then, 'You *could* try it. Transplanting enzymes from a donor *can* be effective with Hurler's Syndrome but, Jules, you're walking a tightrope in these sort of cases. Have you had any experience?'

To Leah seated beside him, it was not hard to guess what the reply had been when Nathan said, 'And that's why you want *me* in on it? It's a while since I came across this kind of thing, but I *have* dealt with it, and so I'll come, by all means. These enzyme defect illnesses are quite horrendous for the patient and the family, and the sooner we get into treatment at gene level the better.' His eyebrows lifted. 'What, tonight?

Fly out tonight? You've already checked the flight times? Er. . .well. . .yes, I suppose I could. If I can catch the flight you mention I will, otherwise I'll be on the next. Have a car meet me, will you, as I shall be tired out by the time I get to you. All right, *oui*, *mon ami*. *Au revoir*.

'You heard all that?' he asked, with a rueful smile.

'Yes, someone is in urgent need of your presence.'

He nodded. 'A young colleague of mine, Jules Lascelles, wants my advice and assistance on a tricky case, which means I'm going to have to fly to Paris as soon as we get back.'

Leah's glow was fast becoming a mere glimmer.

'How long will you be away?'

'Three. . .four days, maybe. Fortunately, I've no complicated surgery planned at this end for a week or so. My assistant can hold the fort at St Bernadette's, and I can rest easy about Barleyfields with you in charge, can't I?'

'Yes, you can,' she assured him sincerely, as the week ahead became an empty void. There was so much she wanted to say to him. . .so much she wanted Nathan to say to her. . .and he was going away.

His bright brown gaze was on her.

'It goes without saying that I shan't delay. I'll be back the very first chance I get.' His voice was wistful. 'I'd planned that we would. . .' He sighed. 'Never mind. What I want to say to you can wait until I get back; you're not going to run away, are you?'

'No, never,' she told him softly, and he gave a satisfied nod.

When they pulled up outside Barleyfields, Nathan took her hand in his, both of them aware that Katie was looking on sleepily.

'I have to dash, Leah,' he said regretfully. 'I've got about an hour to get to the airport.'

She withdrew her hand.

'Are you taking the car?'

He was fishing for his door key.

'No. I'm going to ring for a taxi,' and it seemed that his thoughts were already elsewhere.

The new arrangement of the day staff giving the residents their breakfast was working well, and when Leah went downstairs on Monday morning her team were ready and waiting to start the day.

As Anne Mirfield read the report from the night just gone, Leah was amazed to hear that Mabel had awakened in a happy and tranquil state of mind and immediately asked what was for breakfast.

Once the staff had dispersed, she went to seek her out and discovered that the old lady was indeed much more like her old self.

'You look better, Mabel,' Leah said gently.

'Yes, I *am*, Sister,' she said. 'When I said my prayers last night I told the Lord the same thing that I've been telling him for weeks, that I'm ready to go, but either he wasn't listening, or he has other plans for me. Anyway, for whatever reason, I feel happier this morning. I awoke at seven o'clock and everything seemed brighter. I'd forgotten how lovely the sunshine and the song of the birds are.'

The call came through at ten o'clock. Rupert Curtis had been found dead in his bed by a neighbour, from a massive heart attack, and as Leah took the message she thought that Mabel's surmise had been correct. The Lord *did* have other plans for her, but how would she take the sad news?

'So he's gone, then,' she said matter-of-factly, when Leah told her. 'I wonder if that's why I felt as if a weight had been lifted off my shoulders when I opened my eyes this morning.' Then her face puckered. '*Am* I a wicked old woman, Sister?'

'No, you're not, far from it,' Leah assured her. 'Your

life was spent looking after him. There's no need to feel guilty.'

Mabel gave her old chuckle.

'For the first time I've got one up on him, and as for Tom, he won't be sorry to have heard the last of Whateley's stores. We might get a bit of time to ourselves now.'

There was no word from Nathan, and Leah found herself continually wondering what he was doing and when he would be back. They had been so near to opening their hearts to each other and the moment had gone. Firstly because his concern for her health had overridden their kindling passion, and secondly with the call from France. As a consequence, she felt herself to be in a state of limbo, wondering all the time if he *did* love her, if she had put the right interpretation on what he had said. As she worked in Barleyfields during the day and prowled restlessly around the flat at night, the week dragged on.

On Tuesday afternoon Denise called in to see her and Leah was relieved to see that she seemed to have made a good recovery, and at the same time wondered if her acquaintance from Women's Surgical was wishing she could have her job back.

When she asked her, Denise shook her head.

'No, not really, Leah. I'm reasonably fit now, but not so well that I could come back permanently, even if it were possible. What I had thought, though, was to offer my services as a temp for emergencies and such like. I could cope with that.'

Leah had gone into the kitchen to ask Giles to make a pot of tea for them, but he was nowhere to be seen; only Arthur Conway was there slicing carrots with one of the young cook's sharp knives.

'Arthur! What are *you* doing in here?' she asked sternly. 'What's your wife going to say if you cut yourself badly?'

'That I'm a careless bugger,' he said with a laugh.

'Where's Giles?'

'Gone into the garden for a breather.'

'Does he know you're in here?'

'Yes. I offered to help him and he said OK.'

'I see. Well, do me a favour, will you, Arthur,' she said more gently. 'Keep out of here. The kitchen is out of bounds to residents. If you were to get yourself scalded or burnt, it would reflect on me. I've already had a mini-fire in here and that's enough to be going on with.'

'All right, lass,' he agreed reluctantly, and shuffled off back to his bedroom.

Giles was sprawled on one of the benches soaking up the afternoon sun, and he looked up, startled, when she called his name angrily.

'What's the matter, Sister?'

'You left Arthur Conway in the kitchen doing *your* job, using a very sharp knife. . .that's what's the matter,' she snapped.

He uncoiled himself off the seat.

'Arthur's with-it. He won't come to any harm.'

'That is not the point, as you well know, Giles,' she stormed. 'Patients are banned from the kitchen for their own sakes. Do. . .you. . .understand. . .that?'

'Yes, Sister,' he said with an exaggerated subservience that riled her even more, and loped off to his own domain, leaving her to wonder if she would have been as sharp with him if Nathan had not been out of reach.

Early Wednesday evening the phone rang and Leah leapt to answer it, but the voice at the other end wasn't Nathan's, it was that of her stepmother, Elise, and immediately alarm bells rang.

'Leah, your father's been in an accident,' she said in a high-pitched gabble. 'A girder fell on him on one of the construction sites and he's unconscious in hospital with spinal damage. The doctors won't say if he'll walk again.'

Leah took a deep breath.

'We'll be on the next flight, Elise,' she said immediately, 'but first I'll have to find a replacement here. Fortunately the person who had the job before me has just become available to stand in if needed. If she agrees, there'll be no problem.'

Denise laughed when she phoned her.

'I didn't think I'd be needed so soon! But yes, you go, Leah. I'll take care of everything. . .and I hope there's good news of your dad.'

In the taxi taking them to the airport, Katie burst into overwrought tears and Leah held her close. Their dad could be a pain, but she loved him. . .they both did, and it was unbearable to think of him injured and helpless. Her mind was in a whirl. What would they find when they got to Toronto? And why could Nathan not have been around so that he was aware of the reason for her sudden departure? Any other time he was at her elbow, but not now.

Their flight had been called and as they picked up their hand luggage, Katie's lips began to tremble again. In an attempt to cheer her up, Leah said, 'You'll be able to send a postcard to your two boyfriends.'

'Two?' she echoed.

'Yes, Bobby and Arty,' and as Katie started to laugh, she joined in.

They were still giggling as they boarded the plane. Katie had gone first and Leah had one foot on the aircraft when there was a commotion behind the rest of the passengers waiting to board, and as they parted, Nathan came storming through.

Leah's heart leapt in amazed relief, but only for a second. He took her arm and yanked her off the plane, and as they were jostled to one side, he said furiously, 'Where do you think you're going? I thought I'd left you in charge of Barleyfields! That you would be waiting when I got back, and instead I'm just in time to find you cavorting off to Canada with one big grin on your face! I must have been insane to think we had something special going for us. You've obviously no sense of responsibility, and you know what I think of people like that!'

He paused for breath and she gasped desperately, 'If you'll just let me get a word in I'll explain.'

'Don't bother!' he gritted. 'I can do without excuses.'

'Are you joining us, madam?' a member of the crew asked politely from the doorway and Leah gave an angry nod. He was impossible! And if he thought he could castigate her like this in public, he had another think coming.

She wrenched her arm out of his grasp and stepped back on board, and as she turned, there was an airport official beside him asking if there was a problem, as he had pushed his way through the gate without a ticket.

'No, there isn't!' he snapped. 'I'm going!'

As their glances met, Leah saw distaste in his eyes along with the anger and it was the last straw. Oblivious to the curious stares of those around them, she told him slowly and distinctly, 'I hate you, Nathan!'

Katie had missed the furious confrontation as she had been searching out their seats, and, as Leah had no wish to make her any more miserable, when she slumped into the seat beside her, she made no mention of what had just happened. But she couldn't hold back the tears, and as they rolled slowly down her cheeks it was Katie's turn to console, patting her hand gently, and quite unaware that Leah's bright dream had just been extinguished.

Elise was waiting at the airport and as they hurried anxiously towards her, it seemed to Leah that she was not as fraught as she had expected.

'How is he?' she asked immediately.

'Much better,' Elise told them with a watery smile. 'He's conscious and his spine *isn't* damaged, thank God!'

'So he's going to be all right?' Leah said shakily, as relief swept over her.

'It looks like it, yes,' her stepmother said. 'It's been a dreadful time, and I knew that he would want you both here with him if it did turn out to be serious.' She was eyeing them apologetically. 'Perhaps I should have waited a little longer before dragging you out here.'

Leah managed a smile.

'You did what you thought was best, Elise,' she told her evenly, 'and we want to be here for him, so don't chastise yourself.'

Her stepmother must never know that her agitated phone call had triggered off an explosion that had blown her world apart. An hour later Nathan would have been there. He would have known what had happened and understood. Her mouth tightened. . . Or would he?

Her father was delighted to see them and determined to make light of the accident. He had had a lucky escape, with extensive bruising and shock the only damage, and was expected to be discharged at the end of the week.

'It was worth having a fight with an iron bar if it's brought my daughters to me,' he said with a swollen smile. He looked at Leah. 'You're not going to rush back home again now that you're here, are you? You might as well see something of Toronto. It's an ideal opportunity that mightn't come again, as my stint over here is up in a month and we'll be coming back home.'

Leah heard him out thoughtfully. There was nothing to go home for, as she had already decided that she was not going back to Barleyfields. If that left Nathan in the lurch, he would not be surprised at another instance of her unreliability.

The apartment overlooking the lake was spacious and attractive, and Toronto itself a mixture of grace and ugliness. Its main street was as Katie had described it, sleazy and unattractive in parts, and yet beside the seedy sex shops were elegant shopping malls, and its cosmopolitan population appeared to see nothing strange in the fact.

When they came back from the hospital in the evenings the three of them watched TV or sat out on the terrace above the lake. It was cosy enough, but Leah was restless. She needed to be alone, to sort out her thoughts and plan the bleak future.

There was no one to confide in, as Katie, happy to be back in Toronto because it was only for a visit, would have been worried and anxious about her, and Elise, though a charming woman, was not close enough to her to confide in.

When Leah announced on the fourth day that she was going to take a small trip alone, Katie immediately asked, 'Why can't I come too?'

Leah tweaked her sister's long blonde mane affectionately. 'You've already been where I'm going, and just for once I *do* need to be alone. Dad won't want both of us dashing off.'

'It's Nathan, isn't it?' Katie said. 'You've quarrelled with him, haven't you?'

Leah flinched. It was the understatement of all time.

'Sort off,' she admitted with a bleak smile, and, with that, Katie didn't persist any more.

The hotel on Murray Street was smart and comfortable and only a short distance from the incredible Niagara Falls. As the coach had made its way through the town Leah had been able to see the spray in the distance, hanging over the water in a continuous white cloud. As they stepped out on to the car park, the thunderous roar of the waterfall could be heard above all else.

After she checked in and had a meal, she went into the gardens beside the falls. As she watched the fast-flowing Niagara river hurl itself over the steep drop in foaming pleats that fell endlessly into the surging cauldron below, her eyes stung.

It was a magnificent sight, power and primitive beauty rolled into one, and she had no one to share it with. . .no one with whom to enjoy the unforgettable experience.

A little waitress at the hotel had told her that the water flowed endlessly into the basin that had Canada on the one side and America on the other, and it had only been known to cease when the weather was cold enough to freeze it as it fell, creating huge icy pinnacles that in their immobility might make the observer forget for a moment the huge power that was behind them.

The falls were like Nathan, she thought, a powerful driving force, full of energy and purpose. He could turn to ice in certain conditions, but in his case it wasn't anything to do with the weather.

Her hands gripped the protective rail in front of her. The small boat called *The Maid of the Mist* was battling its way towards the swirling falls, looking small and frail from Leah's position high above on the walkway, and she thought sombrely that was how she had been. . .small and frail, battling against a different kind of force. Well, it was over, safer waters for her from now on, and she turned away miserably, colliding with the man who had come up from behind her.

His hand came out to steady her and Leah sagged with shock.

'Nathan!' she breathed. 'Where? How? Why?'

His smile lacked its usual confidence as he said lightly, 'Where have I come from? Your father's place in Toronto. How did I get here? I flew, after spending days trying to track you down as no one knew your father's address, and why? I think you know *why* I'm here, Leah. It's because I'm a fool, a high-handed jealous fool who's come to ask your forgiveness.'

She sank down on to a low stone wall beside them and looked down at the grass beneath her feet. She could not meet his eyes, not until she had got herself under control, and there was silence between them until she said, 'How *did* you find me?'

As he stood looking down on her, she could see the misery in his eyes. It was the same look she had seen in her own.

'After your plane had left, I went back to Barleyfields and there discovered from the night staff what had happened, that there'd been a crisis in Canada, and you'd arranged for Denise to take your place.'

'But why hadn't they told you all that?' she asked woodenly.

'Because I hadn't even been in the place. My taxi passed yours on the road leading to the home and I was so desperate to be with you, I told my driver to follow yours. When I realised you were heading for the airport, I couldn't believe it. You'd never been out of my mind for a second and I couldn't wait to make up for time wasted. I lost your taxi when we got to the airport complex, and by the time I'd sorted out what flight you were on, you were already boarding, and the hurt in me exploded into rage. That's the truth. I have no excuse. I behaved like a man who's. . .'

'Been hurt once too often?' she finished off for him softly.

He took her hands and brought her to her feet.

'I don't know about that, but what I *do* know is that I love you as I've never loved anyone before. Since I've got to know you, it has seemed as if the world has at last put itself to rights, that there *are* women around whose minds are as lovely as their bodies, and I haven't been able to forget you. It was like having an illness for which there's no treatment when I saw you with that Terry fellow, and the only way I could fight the pain was to criticise and carp at you, when all the time I was thinking that you were the best thing that had ever happened to Barleyfields. . .and me.'

'Shush, Nathan,' she said softly, placing a gentle finger on his lips. 'None of that was necessary. All I need to hear is that you love me. I love you, too, and I respect you as well, your strength and integrity, and the great driving force that is you, It makes me feel humble to know that I've been able to channel that force towards *me*. I only hope that my calmer waters won't put out your fire.'

He gave an incredulous laugh.

'My darling girl, you're the one who lights the fire in me; without you I'm all flame and no heat.'

Leah's eyes went to the falls thundering beside them.

'Before you came, I'd been thinking that the falls are like you.'

He gave a happy grin.

'What? Wet and noisy?'

'No, magnificent,' she said as his arms enfolded her and the strong kissable mouth came down on hers.

MILLS & BOON

LOVE ON CALL

The books for enjoyment this month are:

NOTHING LEFT TO GIVE Caroline Anderson
HIS SHELTERING ARMS Judith Ansell
CALMER WATERS Abigail Gordon
STRICTLY PROFESSIONAL Laura MacDonald

Treats in store!

Watch next month for the following absorbing stories:

LAKESIDE HOSPITAL Margaret Barker
A FATHER'S LOVE Lilian Darcy
PASSIONATE ENEMIES Sonia Deane
BURNOUT Mary Hawkins